Our Forever Love

OUR FOREVER LOVE

PREVIEW FOREVER VOWS

Copyright © 2024 by Kathryn Kaleigh

All rights reserved.

Written by Kathryn Kaleigh.

Published by KST Publishing, Inc., 2024

Cover by Skyhouse24Media

www.kathrynkaleigh.com

No part of this book may be reproduced in any form or by any electronic or mechanical means, including information storage and retrieval systems, without written permission from the author, except for the use of brief quotations in a book review.

This is a work of fiction. Any names, characters, places, or incidents are products of the author's imagination and used in a fictitious manner. Any resemblance to actual people, places, of events is purely coincidental or fictionalized.

ALSO BY KATHRYN KALEIGH

Contemporary Romance

The Worthington Family

The Princess and the Playboy

Forever Vows

Our Forever Love

My Forever Guy

Out of the Blue

Kissing for Keeps

All Our Tomorrows

Pretend Boyfriend

The Forever Equation

A Chance Encounter

Chasing Fireflies

When Cupid's Arrow Strikes

It was Always You

On the Way Home to Christmas

A Merry Little Christmas

On the Way to Forever

Perfectly Mismatched

The Moon and the Stars at Christmas

Still Mine

Borrowed Until Monday

The Lady in the Red Dress

On the Edge of Chance

Sealed with a Kiss

Kiss me at Midnight

The Heart Knows

Billionaire's Unexpected Landing

Billionaire's Accidental Girlfriend

Billionaire Fallen Angel

Billionaire's Secret Crush

Billionaire's Barefoot Bride

The Heart of Christmas

The Magic of Christmas

In a One Horse Open Sleigh

A Secret Royal Christmas

An Old-Fashioned Christmas

Second Chance Kisses

Second Chance Secrets

First Time Charm

Three Broken Rules

Second Chance Destiny

Unexpected Vows

Begin Again

Love Again

Falling Again

Just Stay

Just Chance

Just Believe

Just Us

Just Once

Just Happened

Just Maybe

Just Pretend

Just Because

Our Forever Love

THE ASHTONS

FOREVER AND EVER

KATHRYN KALEIGH

Chapter One

Victoria Graham

It was a rainy Tuesday morning.

A perfect day to stay inside with a hot cup of coffee, a fire in the fireplace, and a good novel.

Instead I stood at the window of my second-floor office in Woodard Hall watching the lightning storm outside. Rain slashed against the window in torrents from the windstorm. The wind whipped between my two-story building and the ten-story building on the other side of the parking lot that separated the two.

The new ten-story engineering building was in stark contrast with this older building that housed the psychology department.

It was a well-known phenomenon that universities always favor the hard sciences over what was considered the softer sciences like psychology, especially when money is involved. And a new ten-story building definitely involved money.

The tunnel effect was one theory about why the wind didn't just howl, but howled with a creepy ghostly noise.

At times anyway.

Like now.

The row of little newly planted oak saplings on this side of the building shivered in the wind. Fifteen of them. Fifteen little transplanted saplings in fresh dirt lined along the sidewalk.

There were older oaks that had survived the new construction on the other side of the building away from the parking lot.

I missed the older oaks that had stood where the parking lot now was. They had stood tall and majestic, their heavy limbs dipping down toward the ground with their weight. Squirrels especially liked scampering among the branches.

I'd watched the protests from my window, but unlike the idealist college students that marched in those protests, I knew that it was futile and progress would win.

I consoled myself and the students who cared by assuring them that we could watch the new oak trees as they grew into their own.

A rumble of thunder shook the glass in the old window. I backed away and sat in my office chair at my desk. I tapped a pencil against my laptop and picked up my cell phone. Checked the radar. Looked like the storm was just getting here.

The power had gone out about ten minutes ago.

It hadn't taken long for the air to go stagnant. I could smell popcorn drifting across the hall from the graduate student lounge. And mixed with that was the scent of wet dog fur. One of the graduate students had a comfort dog that had quickly become the second-year grad student's unofficial mascot.

Leave it to psychology graduate students to adopt a comfort dog as a mascot. They'd even named him Sigmund after Sigmund Freud.

I popped a peppermint in my mouth and leaned back, considering. My class was scheduled to start in fifteen minutes.

The old classroom had nothing more than a hint of a window in the back. Without electricity it would be impossible to see anything.

I could teach without PowerPoint. That wouldn't be a problem. I actually cherished those days when I could go old-school and teach the old-fashioned way—technology free. We always had better classroom discussions on those days.

But today it looked like class was going to be cancelled. Teaching without technology was one thing, but teaching in the dark was another thing entirely. It wasn't that I needed my notes. I didn't need them. I had my lectures memorized. I did, however, need my notes for the two new articles that I wanted to discuss.

Either way, I couldn't very well ask students to take notes in the dark.

I jumped at another rumble of thunder.

I'd wait a few minutes, then go across the hall and give the students the good news. Education was a most baffling phenomenon. It was the one thing people paid for that they actually tried to avoid.

I'd been the same way in college, of course.

And to be truthful, I wouldn't mind going home myself.

Unfortunately, faculty didn't have that privilege. I had a meeting scheduled during lunch and I could use the unexpected time to prepare for it.

My phone chirped with a text message. It was my graduate assistant asking about class today. I wrote her back and told her to stay home until the storm passed.

Standing up, I slid my phone into my pants pocket. I normally wore either a black skirt or black slacks. Today it was pants. There had been no way I was wearing a skirt out in this weather. I wore a long blue tank top under a blue-jean jacket and my waterproof lace-up boots.

Perfect rainy weather attire.

Comfortable enough for dodging raindrops, but not too casual.

I barely reached my door when the student with the comfort dog, a large black lab, at his side stood in front of me.

"Dr. Graham," he said. "Are we having class today?"

"Hi John. Nope. You can head out if you want to. But you might want to let the storm pass first."

"Definitely. Thanks, Dr. Graham. Want me to tell the others?"

"Sure. Go ahead. Just tell them I said to be safe out there."

John would be their hero for the day by bringing the announcement that class was canceled.

He and his dog dashed across the hall. Minutes later fifteen happy graduate students scattered.

Despite my warning, none of them would stay and wait for the storm to pass. It wasn't in their nature.

I walked down the dark hallway to the main office to see if there was any buzz about the university closing. The wind seemed to be getting worse by the minute.

There was a closed sign on the office door and it was locked. I had a key, but I didn't see any reason to use it. Instead, I walked back down the shadowed hall.

Without the graduate students and their lively conversations, the hallway was quiet now.

Too quiet.

I'd been here at the office at night before and that was exactly what this felt like.

Except for the wind.

I went back to my office—the only door open on the long hallway—and shoved my computer into my leather book bag.

The back of my neck started tingling and I had a sudden urge to get out of the building.

It was the howling wind. Creepy. That's what I told myself anyway.

It didn't help that everyone else had vacated the building, leaving it deserted.

It would have been nice to have been in the loop regarding university closures.

I checked my email.

Due to the impending storm and power outage, the university will be closed for the remainder of the day.

Great. Just great.

I'd been sitting here in the dark when I could have been at home by now.

My buddy, Dr. Benson McCoy, was out this week. And since the faculty operated on a modified buddy system, it was no surprise that I'd been left out of the loop.

They'd say it was my fault for not checking my email.

They would not be wrong.

The crash that came next was no rumble of thunder. In fact, it shook the whole building. I grabbed hold of my desk and put an arm over my head to shelter myself from the debris that dusted over my head.

The next thing I knew, there was a tree in the hallway where I'd just walked.

A tree.

It took me a minute to comprehend. Despite the recent tree cuttings for the new building and parking lot, there were still old trees on the other side of the building.

The university, in fact, was known for its historical oak trees. And now one of those historic oak tress had just crashed into the building, landing in the hallway.

My hands shaking, I closed my office door and used my cell phone to call 911.

While I waited for someone to answer, I sat down in my office chair, twirled three hundred sixty degrees, then stood up again.

As calmly as I possibly could, I explained that a tree had fallen into the building.

The dispatcher assured me that someone would be on the way and I should stay put.

The wind was howling in stereo now, both outside the window and on the other side of the door.

Tiptoeing back to the door as though the wind could hear me, I slowly turned the door knob.

With nothing holding it in place now, the wind slammed it back in my direction. I jumped back just in time to avoid being hit by it.

Peeking out the now open door I could see that the tree was indeed across the middle of the hallway. Looking through the limbs, I could see one of the downstairs classrooms. What was left of the desks anyway.

Two thoughts collided in my head.

The first thought was that I needed to get out of here. Woodard Hall was an old building. There could be an electrical fire or a gas leak.

The second thought that came on its heels was that there was no way I was going to get out of here.

The hallway was a cavern. With a tree in it.

With one hand on the door casing, I leaned out just enough to confirm that I wasn't going anywhere.

Putting all my weight against the door, I shoved it closed again and locked it. I don't know what good that would do, but it made me feel better.

I laughed at myself, gallows humor perhaps, for locking out the fallen tree and the wind.

Taking my crossbody bag out of my bottom right desk drawer I draped it over my shoulders. I tucked my phone in the top and zipped it closed.

I sat down again. Took a deep, ragged breath.

My students had gotten out just in time. The classroom where they had been sitting was caved in now.

I'd done everything I could for the moment.

Help was on the way. They'd find a way to get me out of here.

The seconds ticked past. Seconds that seemed like forever.

As the storm raged overhead, I contemplated the death of yet another old oak tree.

Chapter Two

JAMES ASHTON

I stood next to my pickup truck and watched my guys maneuver the firetruck into place.

I'd been back less than two weeks and already the university was falling apart on my watch.

One of the many large, stately oak trees had lost its balance and landed smack in the middle of Woodard Hall. There were tree limbs everywhere.

And a huge hole in the roof with tree limbs protruding from several classrooms and office windows.

It would be a long time before the building was fit for students and professors again. If ever.

A rumble of thunder in the distance offered reassurance that the storm was headed east — away from here.

I didn't smell anything that might indicate fire or a gas leak, but it was an old building and precautions had to be taken.

The only thing other than the distant thunder that I could hear was the firetruck's siren.

Water dripping off the brim of my cap, I glanced at my tablet, sealed in a waterproof cover, and clicked on the message for the third time.

There was no mistaking the words on the screen.

There was a woman trapped on the second floor of Woodard Hall.

Woodard Hall with a tree in the middle of it.

Dr. Victoria Graham.

I knew her. I knew her well.

We had been students together here at the university. In fact, if I remembered correctly, we'd had American History together right here in Woodard Hall.

The new building behind me hadn't been here then. There had been some parking on the road, but mostly it had been a little park area. Benches scattered here and there beneath the old oak trees.

Now the trees were gone and what used to be a park was now a paved parking lot.

Go figure. For a university that discouraged driving on campus, it was rather odd that the old trees had been replaced by parking.

Dr. Victoria Graham.

To me she would always be simply Tori.

Tori and I had been attached at the hip for the last two years of our college undergraduate years.

Then we had simply drifted apart. Tori had gone on to graduate school and I had gone to work for my family.

That had been fifteen years ago. Getting together had gone from being inconvenient to being virtually impossible. She'd been in class or studying. Then she'd been in practicum. Then there was her year long internship in Salt Lake City. That had been the thing that drove the final wedge between us.

I'd heard that she had gotten her psychology license a few years ago. Following a clear and direct path, she had achieved her goal. Still. She was young to be a doctor.

And now she was trapped in her office.

Anybody else and I would have let my men handle this while I stood back and supervised, making sure they didn't miss anything important.

But this was Tori they were talking about.

If anyone was going to rescue her from this predicament, it was going to be me.

I laid my tablet on the seat of my truck and strode over to the fireman holding a ladder, contemplating the best way to get Tori out of there.

"Is Dr. Graham the only one in the building, Sir?" Leo asked, tightening his helmet beneath his chin.

"That's what they tell me."

"I'll just go up and get her, Sir."

'No," I said, putting out a hand to stop him. "I'm going up there."

"But, Sir," Leo insisted. "That's my job."

"I know. But I have my reasons."

Just then Dr. Graham — Tori — appeared at the window.

She was too far away for me to really recognize her. I just had to take dispatch's word for it.

Leo cupped his hands. "Dr. Graham," he yelled. "We're going to get you down safely."

Then Leo proceed to haul the ladder over to prop it against the side of the building.

I returned to my truck, reached inside the open window for the hardhat I kept on the backseat, then pulled on my gloves.

"Move the ladder a bit to the right, Leo," I said as I strode toward the building, securing the strap of the hard hat that replaced my cap.

Leo did as he was asked.

"Can I ask why, Sir?"

"Doesn't matter why," I said, not feeling the need to explain myself as I double-checked the ladder's stability.

"Yes, Sir." But I saw the frown cross his features as I took off up the ladder.

"Don't worry, Leo," I called down. "I take full responsibility."

I laughed to myself at Leo's words whispered under his breath.

"Whatever good that does us."

Leo was right, of course. And later I would explain my reasoning to him. But not now. Right now I had a single-minded focus.

It had been a long time since I had been on a ladder. I felt a little unstable for a second, but it was quickly replaced by that little burst of adrenalin.

It had been entirely too long since I'd gotten out and gotten dirty.

It was only now that I realized I had missed it.

Or maybe my rapid heart rate was in anticipation of seeing Tori again.

We'd had a good thing, the two of us.

I kicked myself as I often did for not trying harder. It hadn't been her fault she'd been so focused. It wasn't like she had avoided me on purpose.

I had never faulted her for being single-minded and I didn't now.

A few feet from the window, I looked up, expecting to see her, but she had stepped away from the window.

Then just as I put a hand on the bottom of the window sill, she was back at the window, her hands on the ledge, looking out.

I felt my right boot slip a little on the damp ladder.

I adjusted my feet, but it was my heart that was slipping.

She shifted her gaze just as I took another step up, putting myself in her line of vision.

Confusion crossed her face, followed by a moment of recognition. Then disbelief. Then shock.

Under other circumstances, the range of rapid emotions on her face might have been amusing.

She took a step back. The disbelief and confusion were back, blended into a charming expression.

I couldn't fault her though. If I hadn't been forewarned by seeing her name on the dispatch order, I would have had a similar reaction.

Considering my current position, balanced on a slippery ladder, I felt fortunate to have the advantage I had.

I grabbed the bottom of the window for stability and grinned at her.

"Hello Tori."

She gasped at the sound of my voice.

"James?"

"At your service."

She blinked. Then put a hand over her eyes and muttered something under her breath about dying. That's what it sounded like anyway.

Not exactly the greeting I had expected.

"It's good to see you, too," I said, climbing inside the window with a little less agility than I would have preferred, especially with Tori watching. It was a harsh reminder that I was no longer in the field for good reason. The younger guys were much better equipped for the physical demands of the job.

Now that I was standing in front of her, she put her hands in her pockets and studied me.

"Why are you here?" she asked.

"Seems you and Leo are on the same wavelength."

Her brow creased in confusion. The same expression she'd worn when she got stuck on a math problem.

"Leo." I nodded toward the window. "My main fireman. I think he expects to have to come and rescue both of us."

She laughed a little at that.

"You're a fireman."

She didn't know. Not her fault. I had not exactly kept in touch.

She couldn't have kept up with me if she had tried. She, on the other hand, had been easy to follow.

"I was," I said, grinning a little sheepishly. "I'm actually the volunteer commander now, but when they told me who was up here, I stepped in to personally get you out of here."

"Oh. Then thank you. I think."

I chose to ignore the last sentence.

"There's a tree in the hallway."

"How'd you know?" she asked with the subtle sarcasm I loved about her.

"Lucky guess." I stepped around her and peeked out the door. "That's gonna be a mess to clean up. You all will have to use a different building."

"I know." She nodded.

"Anybody else up here?"

"I don't think so." She bit her lip the way she always did when she was nervous.

"How'd you manage to get left behind?"

"I missed the memo."

I looked at her a moment. She had that same dry sense of humor I'd known and loved, but she seemed serious about missing the memo.

Then I glanced at her hand. I couldn't help myself.

No ring.

My own wedding band weighed heavy on my hand. When I spoke again, my voice was strained.

"Let's get you out of here."

"Yes. Let's." She nodded, moving toward the window.

"Hold on," I said. "We have to do this the safe way."

Her eyes widened as I removed a strap from my shoulder and stepped toward her.

My own pulse quickened.

Chapter Three

VICTORIA

I couldn't quite get my thoughts together.

James Ashton, my college sweetheart was standing in front of me tying some kind of strap around my waist.

He'd filled out some since I'd last seen him and he stood a full head taller than me. Muscular now. I understood muscular, but taller?

I quickly did the math. It had been right at fifteen years since I'd seen him.

And he smelled good. Like he was fresh from the shower. Not at all how I'd imagined a firefighter might smell — smoky and stale.

He was close enough that I could smell his minty breath. It was good timing that I'd had that peppermint earlier.

I shook my head at the direction my thoughts had gone. We weren't in college anymore. He wasn't going to kiss me.

I didn't fault myself for thinking about him that way. It was to be expected that seeing him would trigger my thoughts to take a familiar, yet dormant path.

My gaze skittered to his lips. How many hours had we spent kissing? More than I could begin to count. I wondered what it would feel like to have those lips back on mine after all this time.

Again. A familiar path.

But instead of kissing me, he tightened the strap, pulling me closer to him.

"Okay," he said. "Now you can go down the ladder."

I had nearly forgotten that he was here to get me out of the building. For a moment, I'd been completely focused on him. Just him.

James Ashton was the last person I expected to see when I'd called 911 to help me get out of this building.

I'd lost touch with him, but the last I knew, he'd taken a job in management working for his family.

But here he was. A commander of a fire department. My local fire department.

I should have known this. I read the paper on occasion. His name would definitely have stood out. But I had missed it.

I had so many questions.

As we moved toward the window, I thought how fortunate we were that the building wasn't on fire and the clouds had moved on, taking the rain with them.

Just seeing him had taken valuable time for me to orient.

He had the other end of the strap that I was wearing around his own waist. He helped me climb over the window and put my feet on the ladder.

I'd never been fond of ladders.

But knowing that he was holding onto the strap around my waist, I knew I was safe. It also helped that his hands were beneath my shoulders.

"Coming down," he called out to those below.

I kinda figured they could see that, but it was no doubt some kind of fireman protocol.

As I descended the ladder, he let out the rope as I went.

When I was on the second to the last step another fireman swept me from the ladder and held me steady until my feet were planted firmly on the ground.

I slowly blew out a breath.

"You okay, ma'am?"

"Yes." I nodded and looked up as James stepped over the ledge. I held my breath until his feet were on the ground, too.

"Thanks, Leo," James said. "I've got it from here."

Leo went about the business of taking down the ladder and carrying it back to the fire truck. Mumbling something under his breath, he shook his head.

"You don't normally go up ladders, do you?"

He grinned. "Today seemed like a good day to make an exception."

I smiled back, biting my lower lip. I supposed it would be like me taking over a counseling session for one of the students I supervised for no obvious reason and no warning.

"I need to fill out some paperwork," he said. "Come with me."

I followed him to the unmarked white pickup truck.

"Of course." I nodded. If there was one thing I knew about, it was paperwork.

What I hadn't expected, though, was the course of disappointment that ran through my veins. He only wanted me for the paperwork.

"It was good to see you," I said and I meant it.

He tossed his hat into the backseat of his truck then turned and looked at me for a moment. The wind tossed a lock of hair across his forehead. With an absent gesture, he swept it back.

I wasn't sure what I was supposed to do. He wasn't giving me any indication that I should either stay or go. Did he need me for the paperwork?

"Um," I said. "My car's around on the other side of the building."

"That can't be good," he said, making a face.

"True," I said, a sinking feeling in the pit of my stomach as I realized that my car could have been damaged in the storm.

"You should give us time to check things out. Make sure it's safe."

"Right." How had I seriously not thought about that? With a tree in the middle of the building, there was no way to know what the other side of the building looked like.

Damn it. I'd been okay with the building being torn apart. That was work. It was ultimately someone else's responsibility. My car was a different story. I'd only had my little Camry for less than a year.

Another truck, similar to James's pulled up and parked a few yards away. The driver, a heavyweight man, got out and walked toward the firetruck.

"Actually," James said. "There's not much we can do at the moment. Can I take you to lunch?"

Old memories flooded back in a flash. All those nights sitting in a pizza parlor, studying our respective textbooks.

Lunches in the student center.

Looking back, I seriously believed that having a boyfriend... girlfriend as the case may be, added significant value and depth to one's college experience.

It was a sentiment I often kept to myself, especially among colleagues who frowned upon the whole college relationship thing. So many professors believed that college was a time to explore and be free.

My exploration had been much more freeing by having someone to share it with.

"Yes," I said before I talked myself out of it.

It seemed a little unusual for him to leave right now.

"Great." His face lit up with a smile.

I had so many questions. So many things I wanted to know about my college boyfriend who was now a man.

And something about the intensity of his gaze suggested that he, too, had questions about me.

I smiled back.

James opened the passenger door of his truck and waited for me to come stand next to him. As I stood wondering how I was going to climb inside the truck that was much further off the ground than my car, he held out his hands.

As I put one foot on the running board, he grabbed my waist and before I knew what was happening, he'd lifted me safely onto the seat.

I caught my breath. This was a James I wasn't familiar with. A take-charge, confident James. He'd always been a gentleman, but this was different somehow.

I liked it. But then how could I not like the man that I had played such a part in molding from the youth I'd spent so very much time with?

After closing my door, he went around and climbed into the driver's seat. Started the motor.

"Pizza?" he asked.

It was as though he had read my mind.

"Sounds better than the student union."

He laughed. "Yeah. We spent a lot of time there, didn't we?"

"The student union. The pizza parlor." My apartment. I wasn't quite ready to remind him about that.

Just in case he'd forgotten.

Before putting the truck in gear, he reached over, squeezed my hand.

"It's so good to see you, Tori."

My heart did a little flutter.

How was it that such a destructive storm put James back in my life?

That was something I would have to think about later.

Right now, I focused on staying in the moment.

On enjoying the moment with my college sweetheart from so long ago.

I encouraged my students to accept the role of fate in their lives. Most of them were strong proponents of free will and all the implications that went with that.

I didn't disagree with any of those sentiments.

But accepting that fate played a role in everyone's life helped to instill an added dimension to their lives that spilled over into their therapeutic relationships.

Once people realized that they couldn't control everything, there were things in life that seemed to get a little bit easier to accept.

James backed truck out and pulled out onto the main road automatically heading toward the old pizza parlor.

I had accepted a long time ago that James would no longer be a part of my life. That had been hard for me to accept and had been a long road.

And now, I was willing to accept that James Ashton was destined to be a part of my life. So easy to accept and so fast.

Apparently, with it being that easy to fall back into accepting him as a part of my life, I hadn't been as over him as I had convinced myself to be. I'd given it a good shot. I'd pretended to be over him until I believed it.

I could admit to myself how very much I'd missed him all these years.

We turned toward downtown and I smiled as he pulled up in front of the pizza parlor.

Some things in life came full circle.

And this was one circle that I was more than willing to explore.

As he put the truck in park and grabbed his cell phone from the dash, I saw the glint of a ring I hadn't noticed before.

James was wearing a wedding ring.

Resignation washed over me.

Of course he was married.

A handsome man like James would be married.

He and I had talked about it. Like a lot of guys, he hadn't been opposed or afraid of commitment.

It just made sense that he was married.

"Ready?" he asked.

"Sure." I forced a smile.

I'd allowed myself a moment of fantasy. A moment of what could have been. Everyone did it at some point. I knew a lot of people who used social media to explore new relationships with old flames.

I guess I was an overachiever. I chose to explore my old relationship in vivo.

"I'll come around," he said.

I couldn't remember the last time a man had opened the car... or truck... door for me.

James had not been like any of the other men I had dated after him.

He'd set an impossibly high standard, one I didn't expect anyone to meet.

A little taller. A little more muscular. But if anything, he was more handsome.

His hair was still a dark brown. His eyes still the blue of the deepest, clearest ocean.

And he still had that same easy smile he'd always had.

I pushed away the regrets that washed over me. There was nothing I could do about him being married.

It was one of those fate things.

I sighed.

I had to heed my own advice and accept the role of fate in my life.

Chapter Four

JAMES

After the hostess, a peppy college girl with a high blonde ponytail, led us to a booth at the back of the pizza parlor, I slid into the booth across from Tori.

The red and white checkered table top was faded with age. Probably the same table tops that were here fifteen years ago.

There was something comforting about the scent of pizza. Maybe it was the memory of spending time in here with Tori. Memories of happy times.

Since it was barely eleven o'clock, the place wouldn't start getting crowded for another hour.

I clasped my hands together on the table in front of us and caught the glint of my wedding ring.

Well hell.

I slid my hands off the table and wondered if Tori had noticed.

I hardly even thought about it anymore.

"How are you?" I asked, wondering if it was too late to pull the ring off. Or would that be taken the wrong way?

"Considering I just had a tree fall into my building, I guess I'm okay."

The server came to our table and we ordered cokes.

"How is it that you were able to just leave the scene back there?" she asked.

"Did you notice the guy who drove up as we left?"

"Yeah. The heavy set guy."

"He's the chief."

Tori frowned. "I thought you were the chief."

"I'm a volunteer. Chief of volunteers."

"I see. So there's some friction there."

I sat back. Once a psychologist. Always a psychologist. She'd cut her psychological teeth on me. Truly. I should be used to it.

"Something like that," I said.

She nodded slowly. "I'm glad you were there anyway."

"Me too. It was fortuitous."

"Yes," she said with a smile. "Fortuitous."

"How's the university world?"

"It's good," she said, leaning back. "I like the students. Not so much the other faculty."

"They can be snotty and narcissistic."

"How do you know this?" she asked.

"I have a sister who's adjunct. Charlotte. And the narcissistic part I learned from you."

She looked at me with her head tilted to the side.

"Charlotte is a professor?"

"Teaches art at one of the colleges in Pittsburgh."

She nodded slowly.

"I can see that. Wouldn't have thought it, but I can see it."

"She loves it."

"You remember learning about narcissism from me?"

I grinned.

"I was your first student, remember?"

"I do remember."

"Do you still think that's the best way to learn? By teaching others?"

"Absolutely. It's the only reason I know more than my students."

"I doubt that's the only reason you know more."

She shrugged.

"I'm surprised, but glad, to hear that you remember some of it."

"I remember a lot of things," I said.

Right now the thing that concerned me the most was that I hadn't looked Tori up before now.

I'd known where she was.

But the idea of just showing up at her office seemed too awkward.

I shouldn't have let a little awkwardness keep me from her.

I'd been afraid. I'd been afraid she was with someone.

I preferred to imagine her out there teaching, going home, spending her evenings reading. Living a quiet life.

Living the life she would have lived with me if I hadn't let time and space drive a wedge between us.

A whole lot of water had passed under that bridge.

Our lives had diverged and yet it seemed that fate had seemed fit to bring our paths back together again.

Fate was a funny thing, but there was no denying it.

None whatsoever.

"Does Charlotte like being an adjunct?" she asked, steering the conversation away from us.

She'd done it on purpose. Tori did everything on purpose.

None of her conversation topics were random. She always had a reason for whatever she said.

She'd seen the ring. I'd put money on it.

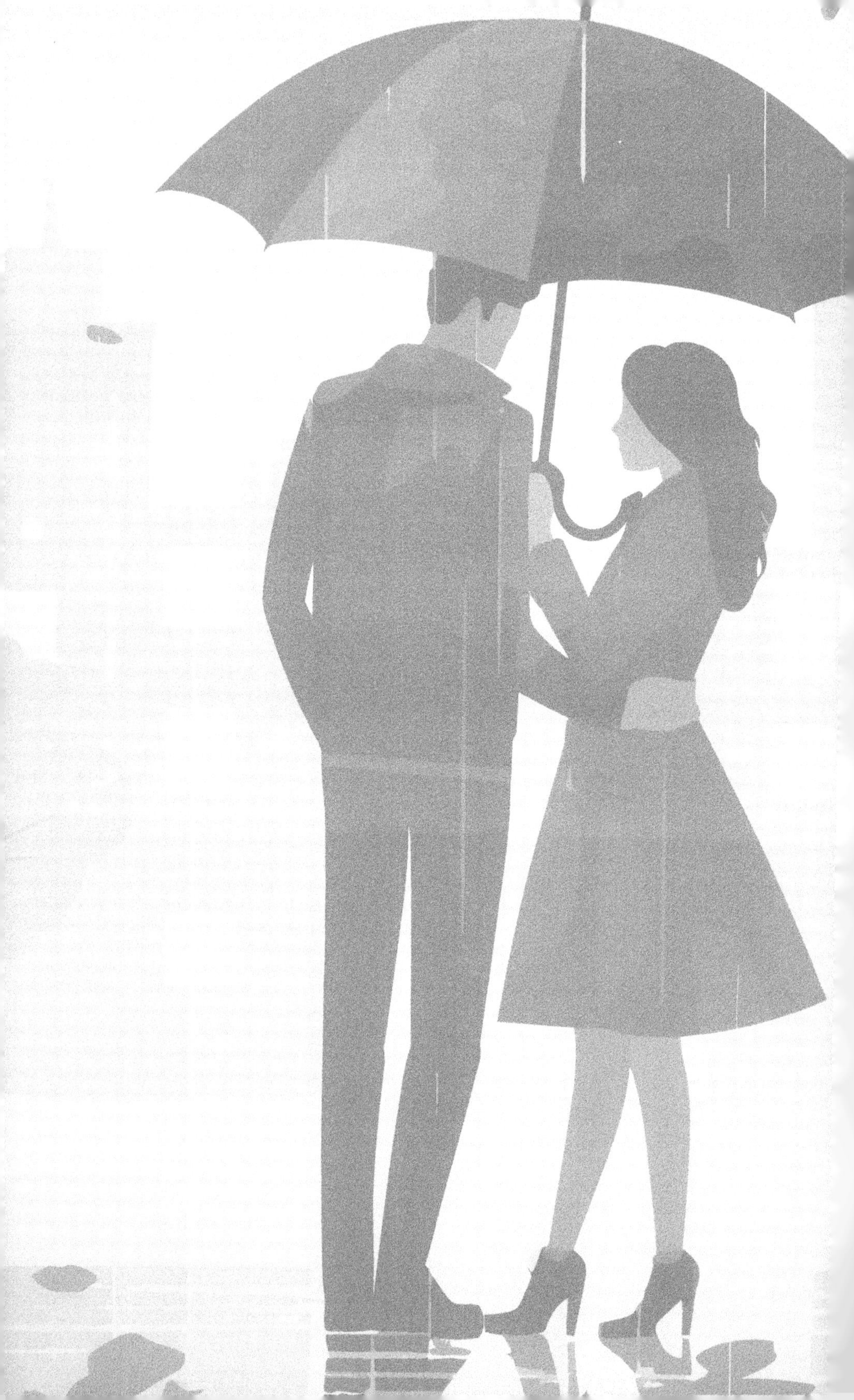

Chapter Five

VICTORIA

The pizza parlor hadn't changed much in fifteen years. I'd order delivery from here, but I hadn't actually eaten here. Not since James.

It was one of those purposeful avoidances. Perhaps unconscious but still an avoidance.

"Charlotte likes being an adjunct. She likes that she doesn't have to deal with meetings with snotty faculty. It gives her some time to paint. Not as much as she would like, but some."

"Not dealing with snotty faculty meetings is definitely one of the few benefits of being adjunct."

"Few?"

"Underpaid. Overworked."

"More than full-time faculty?"

"In some ways, yes," I said. "The education system is broken."

"And yet you stay in it."

"I can't think of anything else I'd rather do."

He nodded slowly. "I get that."

One of the servers came and took our order.

"You still like pineapple and black olives?" James asked me.

"Wow. Good memory."

"Hard to forget," he said with a grin. "You're the only person I've ever met who eats that particular combination."

"How did you end up being a firefighter?" I asked. "I thought that was just a childhood thing."

"Guess it was more than that," he said. "Volunteer."

"Volunteer. Sort of like being adjunct."

He laughed. "Sort of."

"So you must do something else, too. I can't imagine an Ashton not having full days."

"Interesting observation, Dr. Graham."

And one he avoided answering.

"Since you majored in aviation and your father was a pilot at one time, I can only surmise that you might be a pilot."

"Henry's a pilot, too."

"Henry? No. He's not old... enough... Never mind." Henry was James's youngest brother and James was the oldest of five siblings. Three brothers with two little sisters.

"Time flies, doesn't it?"

"Yes," I said, remembering the ring on his finger.

He kept his hands beneath the table. That told me he didn't want to talk about it.

I was okay with that. I didn't want to talk about his wife either.

"I think you're avoiding answering the question."

"Yes," he said. "I do some flying for Skye Travels."

"Skye Travels. They have planes in Pittsburgh?"

"Some," he said. "Noah Worthington never misses a chance to expand his company."

"I see," I said, looking into his eyes. "I get the feeling there's more to that story."

"Your feeling would be right."

The server dropped our pizza off and James slid a piece on one plate for me and another for him.

"Are you going to tell me or do I have to figure it out?" I asked.

"I'll have to tell you. You would never in a million years figure this one out."

"You don't have much faith in my abilities."

"I have plenty of faith in your abilities. But in this particular case, I don't think anyone could come close."

I took a bite of the hot cheesy pizza and tried to come up with something witty to say.

Instead, my thoughts kept circling around to the wedding ring on his finger.

I wondered how long I could go without asking him about it and issued myself a personal challenge to not ask him. He would tell me when he was ready. Besides, it was none of my business.

"My grandfather and Noah Worthington are brothers."

I nearly dropped my slice of pizza and I literally felt my jaw drop.

"No way."

"Like I said." He shrugged.

He was right. There was no way I would have figured that one out.

Not in a million years.

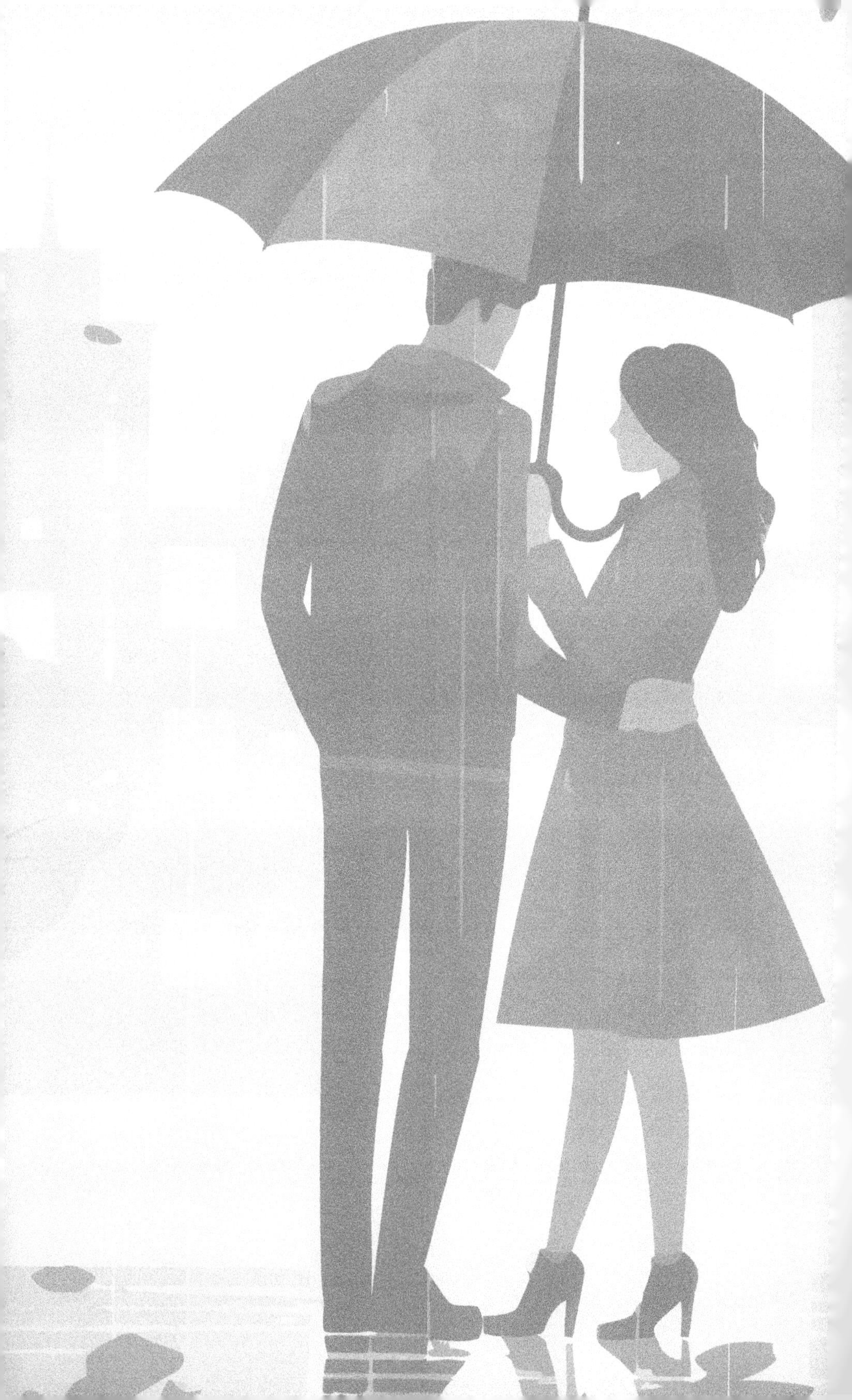

Chapter Six

JAMES

It had been fifteen years since I'd had a black olive and pineapple pizza, but it was good. Better than I remembered.

Nostalgia, I told myself.

"Wait," Tori said, putting both hands on the edge of the table in front of her. "They don't have the same last name. Ashton. Worthington."

"You're taxing your brain for no reason," I said. "Grandpa changed his name. It's a long story. I'll tell you sometime."

"I'd love to hear it," she said. "Curiosity is getting the best of me."

"Later," I said, checking my phone. "I've only got another thirty minutes before I have to head to the airport."

"You have a flight?"

"Got to fly a fellow over to Philadelphia."

"How do you balance everything?"

I shrugged.

"When I'm here I take volunteer calls. Like the one that came in today from the university. There's a whole network of volunteers around the city so they don't notice when I'm not here."

"I never gave that much thought."

"You're not alone in that."

"It's very impressive though," she said. "And you supervise them?"

"Mostly I do training."

"Education runs in the family."

"Actually," I said. "I attribute that particular propensity to you."

"You give me a lot of credit."

"You influenced me during my formative years."

She laughed.

"You're not wrong," she said. "But it was there all along." She leaned forward. "You like that adrenaline rush."

"And," I said, echoing her words. "You're not wrong. I used to. But now. Not so much. I think I got all that out of my system before I turned thirty."

"Good for you."

"You don't think I'm turning into a dull older man?"

"You? You don't have a dull bone in your body."

She was letting me steer the conversation back to us. Where I wanted it.

But now that we had, I found myself backing away from the precipice.

I wasn't ready to talk about myself. I wanted to hear about her.

She wasn't wearing a ring. Didn't mean she didn't have a boyfriend.

Or an ex. I didn't consider myself an ex. She and I had never been engaged.

Should have been, I realized with a start.

Sitting here with her in front of me, put things in a whole new light.

She'd barely changed at all except that she looked more elegant and calm. The calm would be the professor in her.

She still had shoulder length brunette hair. Wore just the right amount of makeup to accent her dark green eyes and high cheek bones. A touch of lip gloss to highlight those bow shaped lips that knew how to curve into a kiss.

The male students would love her and the female students would want to be her.

It had always been that way with her.

Some girls made other girls jealous, but Tori had a wholesome, nonthreatening quality about her that made other girls want to be like her.

My two younger sisters were no exception to that.

Charlotte, the quiet one, never said anything, but my youngest sister, Isabella, still to this day, tossed out Tori's name now and then when she was making a point about my love life.

Typical younger sister.

"The family would love to see you," I said before I thought it through.

"Sounds like your family has had plenty of drama," she said. "Finding out your grandfather has a brother."

"They can handle it," I said, glancing at my phone.

I really did have to leave for my flight, especially if I was going to drop Tori back off at the university.

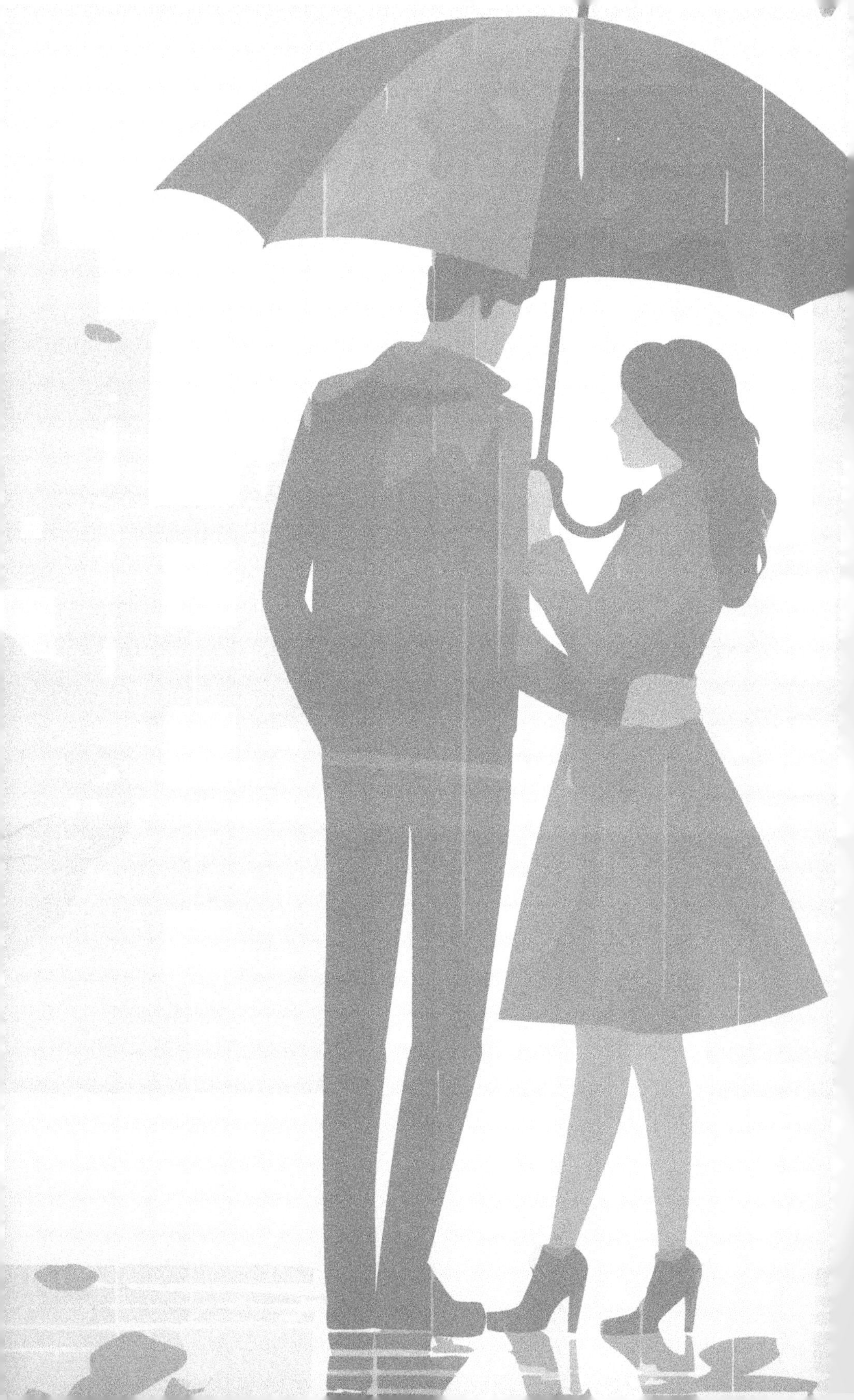

Chapter Seven

VICTORIA

James was confusing me.

As we sat waiting for the server to bring his credit card back, I tried to sort things out.

He wanted me to see his family. It hadn't been a straight out invitation. More like a testing the waters invitation. But a married man didn't bring another girl around his family.

Questions. I had questions.

But I was sticking to my challenge.

Not that it was much of a challenge. I knew I could do it.

I'd worked with clients where I had to go several sessions waiting for them to figure something out for themselves. Sometimes I wanted to just shout at them. But shouting was not a proven therapeutic technique.

So I learned to wait it out.

I could do it.

We left the pizza parlor and went back out to his truck.

The rain was gone now and the sun was out. It was almost like the storm had never happened.

Reaching the passenger door of his truck, I grabbed hold of the door and hoisted myself onto the seat before he could pick me up and put me inside.

He just lifted an eyebrow as he closed the door and went around to the driver's seat.

As he backed out onto the street, I noticed that his ring was gone now.

He'd pulled it off.

Should that have made me feel better?

It actually made me feel worse and even more confused.

He had a good reason, I was certain of it.

I tried to come up with some possible reasons.

Maybe his wife had died.

Maybe he had a child and didn't want to confuse the child.

Maybe he wore it for something work related.

"Do you want me to take you home?" he asked. "Or do you want to see how your car did?"

"My car," I said. "I have to deal with it sometime. Might as well be now."

"You never were one to put things off," he said.

I couldn't tell if he was complimenting me or not.

Either way, he was right. I hadn't gotten where I was now by putting things off.

Closed for the day, the university was deserted. In fact, my car was the only car in the parking lot on the side of the building.

Wind from the storm that had gone through had somehow pulled the several hundred year old oak tree up by the roots, exposed now, and dropped it over the top of the building.

Guys in yellow vests and chainsaws walked around cutting some of the smaller limbs off and stacking it all to the side. The buzz of their chainsaws loud even inside the truck.

"It looks like a tornado went through," I said.

"Might have touched down. Or maybe a straight line wind."

Since the tree seemed to be the only damage, only being a relative term considering the extent of the damage, I was inclined to agree with the straight line wind theory. I'd seen the swatch of damage from a tornado before and this wasn't it.

"I take it that's your car," he said.

It wasn't hard to figure out that the only car in the parking lot was mine.

From here my little white Camry looked unscathed and was parked about as far away from the fallen tree and all the activity that went along with it as possible.

I'd been lucky.

"Thanks for the pizza," I said. "And the ride."

He pulled up next to my car and parked.

"I'd like to see you again," he said.

My heart skipped a beat. Maybe two.

"Are you sure that's a—"

His phone started ringing.

"It's my client," he said. "I'll call him right back."

Opening his door, he hopped out and came around to open my door.

I slid out. He touched my elbow to steady me. I didn't realize I needed to be steadied until I looked into his clear ocean blue eyes.

I blinked, my thoughts scattering.

He made a noise, a sound somewhere between a groan and a growl, and pulled me into a hug.

As he wrapped his arms around me and pulled me close, my arms automatically went around him, too.

He smelled familiar and different all at once. Clean. Like he was freshly showered and, maybe I imagined it, but I detected a hint of jet fuel.

Mostly being in his arms felt like being home.

I sighed, feeling safe. Safer than I remembered feeling in a long time.

About a million thoughts went through my head at one time, none of them making a lot of sense.

I shifted back a little, but he just held on tighter.

Only then did I remember the ring on his finger.

I couldn't make sense of it, but he needed to go. Now was not the time to bring it up.

Then he released me, kissed me on the forehead, and took my hand to lead me toward my car.

It automatically unlocked as we neared the door and he opened my door.

The buzzing of the chainsaws prohibited any conversation, not that I could put two thoughts together anyway.

After I was inside, he closed the car door and just like that, he was gone.

Sitting in the relative silence of my car, I watched him walk around his truck and climb inside.

I was still sitting there as he drove off.

A surreal moment in time. A chance encounter with James Ashton.

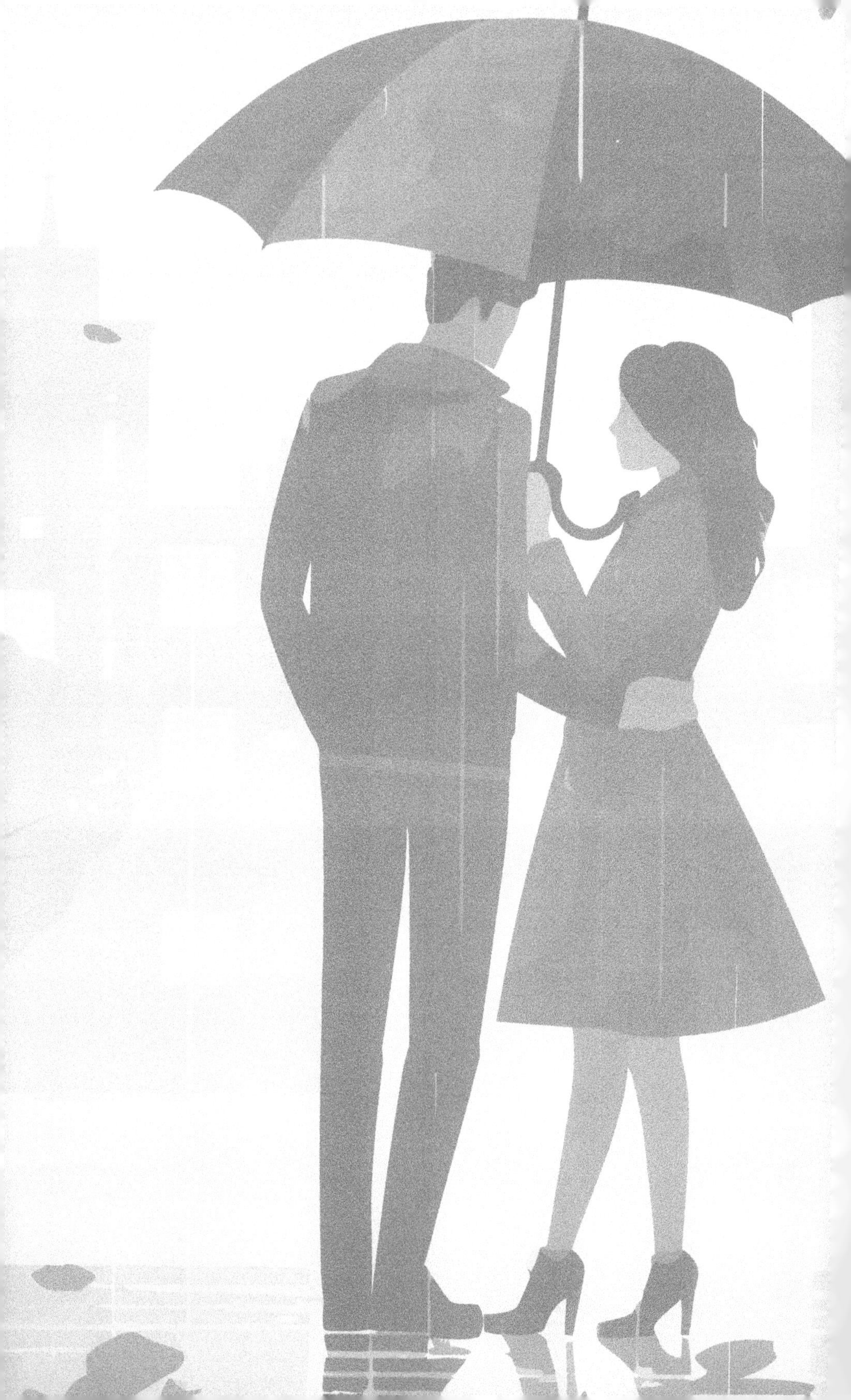

Chapter Eight

JAMES

After getting my passenger, Mr. Sylvester Martin, settled into the plane, I went into the cockpit and went through the preflight checklist.

A lot passengers liked to sit in the copilot's seat, but not Mr. Martin. He liked to work in the back. In fact, one of his requirements was to have WIFI in the airplane, no matter how short the trip.

I was still feeling a little stunned after so fortuitously running into Tori. And not just running into her, but being the one to rescue her. Not a burning building, but a building nonetheless.

Seriously, what were the odds?

It wasn't chance. I was sure of that.

There was most certainly something more than chance at work to have our paths cross again.

Then there was the matter of my wedding ring.

I only wore it when I was around the guys. One of the firemen I worked with, Daryl, had tried to warn me that it wouldn't work.

He'd been right. Scarily right.

But I wasn't ready to admit it to him.

As long as I wore the wedding ring, he left me alone about it.

I'd known it wasn't going to work. I'd known it just as sure as the world.

It especially became clear to me on the flight out to Vegas for the wedding.

Eloping had been Tiffany's idea. Her small family wasn't close and she didn't want to have a wedding with no one sitting on her side.

My assurances that it didn't have to be that way didn't work.

So despite my too little too late realization that the wedding was a mistake, the whole thing had been like a train I couldn't stop.

I'd liked her well enough. I just didn't love her.

I knew I was in trouble, when I found my thoughts straying to Tori.

More specifically when I'd called her Tori. Out loud.

Fortunately Tiffany hadn't caught it. She'd chalked it up to me being tongue-tied.

The wedding ring burned in my pocket.

It was probably a good thing we were in an airplane and not a car.

If I'd been in a car, I probably would have flung it out the window.

Tori, bless her heart, hadn't said anything, but she'd seen it. There was no way it was possible that she hadn't.

And now I would have to explain it to her.

I'd have to tell her about Tiffany anyway, but this just made it harder.

It was such a simple explanation.

But after she got home and thought about it, she might think of me as some kind of scumbag who cheated on his wife.

Hell, I'd felt like I was cheating on Tori when I was with Tiffany.

That was part of why I went ahead with the wedding. I was pushing myself to get past Tori. There was no sense in pining after someone for fifteen years. It was time to move on.

Turns out my gut was right.

There was no one else like Tori. Never had been. Never would be.

I'd probably confused the hell out of her when I'd mentioned seeing my family again.

What man wearing a wedding ring took a girl, even his college sweetheart, maybe especially his college sweetheart, home to his family?

I'd been stupid and stubborn and maybe even a little bit chicken by not already seeking Tori out when I knew where she worked.

But now that I'd been given a second chance, I wasn't going to let it slip by. I was going to see her again.

And this time I wasn't going to let her go.

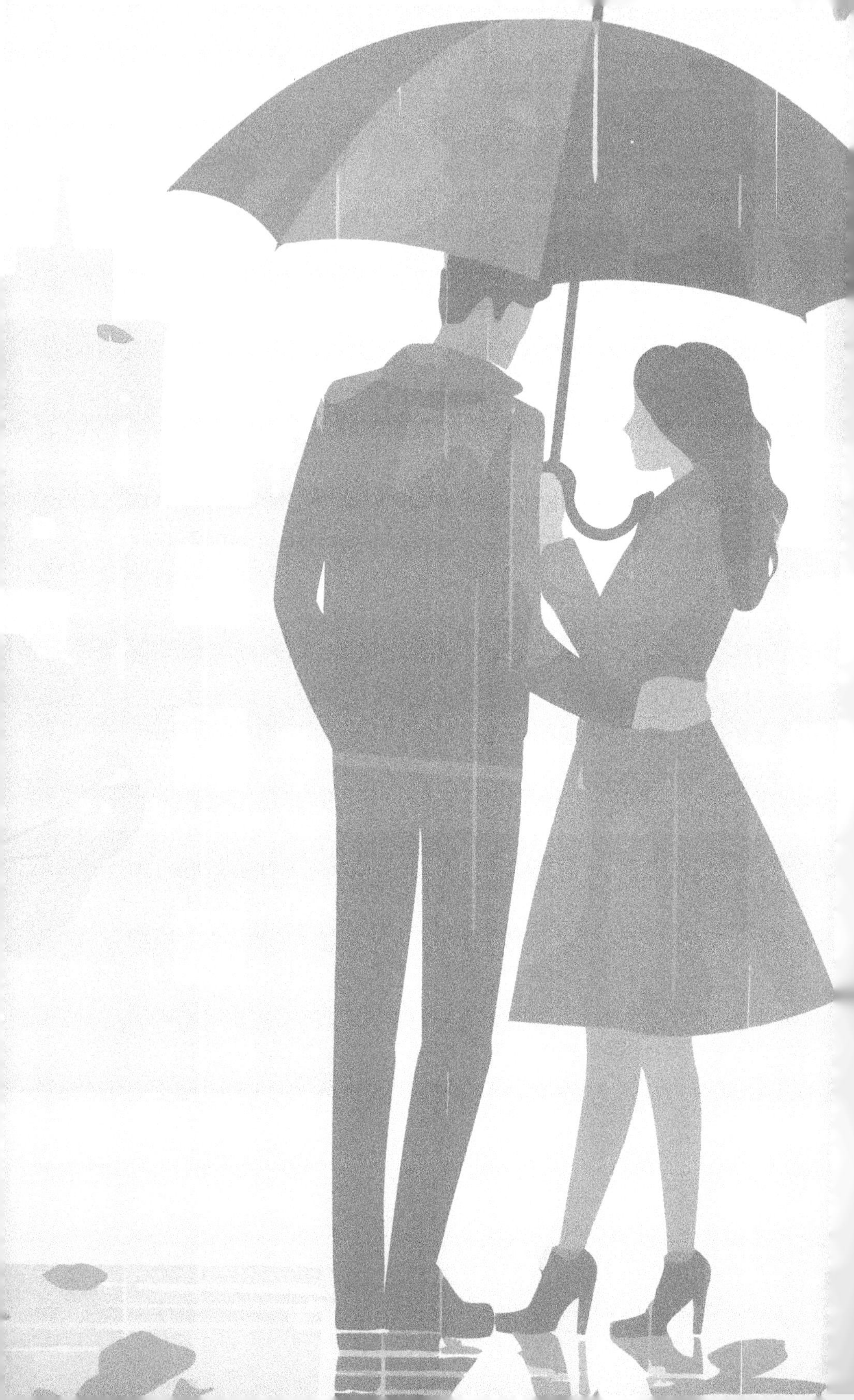

Chapter Nine

VICTORIA

It took a week for the administration to figure out what to do with us.

Woodard Hall was condemned.

As an icon on campus, people grieved it almost as much as they grieved the old oak trees.

We moved our classes online for that week of transition and chaos.

Sitting in my new temporary office, I swiveled around in my office chair and looked out the window of my third floor office. Even though it was temporary, I was pretty sure I would have this office for at least the rest of the semester.

Then over the summer break someone would figure out what to with the homeless psychology department.

Everything felt off-kilter. Even the students were walking around looking out of sorts.

The sidewalks below were crowded with first semester freshmen, sophomores, juniors, and seniors.

They all had their own look and I could usually tell them apart with no more than a glance.

The freshmen had a look between lost and a little excited. They carried their books in backpacks and wore college logo t-shirts. They looked younger and could pass for high school students.

The sophomores usually carried laptops with them, no books, and although they still looked young and fresh faced, they had a more relaxed look. They usually wore a serious, studious look.

The juniors usually carried an iPad and fewer books. They were even more relaxed than the sophomores. A junior rarely came to class in their sweatpants. Able to see the light at the end of the tunnel, they dressed more professionally.

Seniors typically exuded a devil may care attitude. Confident and older.

I spotted John walking along with Sigmund. Only a graduate student would have the confidence to walk the campus with a dog, especially since Sigmund wore a vest or a coat or a shirt, whatever it was, identifying him as a comfort dog.

Sigmund garnered some looks, but to their credit, no one stopped to pet Sigmund. It was our culture. Kids today had grown up in a world where comfort and service dogs were considered normal and they were taught not to distract them by playing with them.

Since I taught both graduate and undergraduate, I had my feet in both worlds. It was amazing how much more advanced the graduate students were than the undergrads.

For once I was just thankful that my graduate students had not heeded my advice during the storm. If they had stayed like I suggested, they would have been hurt.

I turned away from the window and opened my computer.

Transitioning from face to face classes to online classes and back again could be a challenge.

Had it been up to me, I would have kept the undergrads online for the rest of the semester. There were only five weeks left and one of those was finals.

The graduates, though, needed to be face to face in order to role play. We did a lot of role plays. It was how I had learned best in school, as early as undergrad, and I passed that along to my students.

My self-generated undergrad role plays had consisted solely of James. Mostly I had role played explaining things to him so I role played being a professor, even though I hadn't known it at the time.

I wasn't always going to be a professor. Not at first. At first I wanted to work in a mental hospital. I'd done that when I was in Utah for a year.

But I'd found myself teaching things during both group sessions and individual sessions. That's when I realized I wanted to teach—all the time.

And oddly enough, I now taught graduate students how to do counseling.

I opened my notes, but I instead of reviewing them, I just stared at the words on the screen.

James said he wanted to see me again.

Perhaps it had been a passing impulse. A week had gone by and I hadn't heard from him.

He didn't have my cell phone number and since I wasn't in my usual office, he wouldn't be able to use the college directory to find me here.

I was lost to him.

I, on the other hand, had the advantage. I'd found his name on the Skye Travels website.

Even though I didn't call it and didn't plan to, I'd put the phone number to Skye Travels in my phone.

It was comforting having it there.

Comforting knowing that I knew where to find him.

Since I didn't have a good reason to call him at work, I didn't do it.

I glanced at my watch. It was time for me to start making my way across campus for class. The office I had been assigned was nowhere near the classroom they had given us. I didn't even want to think about what kind of nightmare it must have been to find space for all the classes that had been displaced.

The only good thing about the room they'd put me in was that it had no multimedia capabilities. I would be teaching using a white board and markers.

I honestly believed that I was a better professor teaching the old-school way. It took longer, sure, to write things on the board than to flash them on the screen. But sometimes slowing down could be a good thing.

I put my computer in my leather book bag. I might not need it, but I'd be lost without it, grabbed a bottle of water, and headed out.

I made it to the other side of my desk.

James stood there in the doorway.

"Hi," he said.

"Hi." My heart rate skittered into an erratic beat.

"You're headed to class," he said.

"Yes. How did you find me?"

"I have my ways," he said with a grin.

I nodded slowly. James Ashton had always had ways.

It occurred to me in that moment that he could have found me years ago if he had wanted to.

My question, which I kept to myself, was why now.

"Can I walk you to class?" he asked.

"Sure," I said. I didn't even try to pretend that I didn't want him to. At thirty-six years old, I considered myself past the age of playing games.

"Then you have to let me carry your books."

"Except we don't carry books anymore."

"Kids today don't know what they're missing," he said. "Your computer then."

I handed him my computer bag.

Why not?

I might be thirty-six, but I wasn't too old to appreciate having the man I'd been crushing on my whole life walk me to class and carry my computer bag.

"I heard they condemned Woodard Hall," he said. "It was an icon."

"They did. First they cut down the old oak trees and now they condemned the old building. Nothing is sacrosanct."

We walked down the hallway crowded with students toward the stairs. Having one building out of commission messed with the ecosystem of all the others on campus.

"It's the way the world works," he said. "Want to use the elevator?"

"No thanks," I said, with a little shudder. "It needs to be condemned. It's constantly getting stuck." Besides, I had worn my sneakers today, knowing I was going to have to walk across campus.

If I had known I was going to see James today, I might have worn different shoes. Probably not heels. Maybe boots.

It was okay though. With me wearing sneakers, the top of my head barely came to James's shoulders. Either he had gotten taller or he held himself taller.

Or maybe I was simply more aware of him.

Back when we were in college, we were used to each other. Together all the time.

We went to his grandparents' house just about every Sunday. His family was big on tradition. Spending Sunday afternoons together was one of those traditions.

James had two younger brothers and two little sisters. The youngest sister always brought a friend. Sometimes his brothers brought a friend or a girl. Sometimes even the neighbors would stop by.

It was a whole lot different from the way I had grown up. I had one older brother who was already living in Boston practicing as an attorney by the time I was a teenager. My parents, also attorneys, worked all the time, so I rarely saw them after I moved away to college.

I didn't have girlfriends, not close ones anyway.

I had been content with James.

We made our way down the crowded stairs, down six flights of stairs, to the bottom floor and stepped out into the fresh air.

"Where is your class?" James asked.

"Dobb's Hall," I said, wrinkling my nose. The soft autumn wind tousled my hair. I shoved it back, holding it back with one hand.

"I'm surprised they haven't condemned that building already."

"They need to," I said. "They haven't spent any money on upgrading it."

"Sometimes it takes a tree," he said.

"Maybe."

As he shifted my bag on his shoulder, I noticed that he was not wearing a ring.

I almost wanted to believe that I had imagined it.

But I knew I had not.

"It's sort of like the old days, isn't it?" he asked.

"A little," I said.

Back when we were college students, though, I had felt secure with him. I'd known what we had planned from one day to the next. From one week to the next.

That was not the case now.

I didn't know what to expect from one minute to the next. The fact he was here right now walking me to class was a surprise in and of itself.

I missed those days when I hadn't had to worry about whether or not we were going to have dinner together. I had known we would, even if it was just a sandwich from the student union, eaten while we read and studied.

He and I'd had an easy companionship.

I definitely missed it.

"Hey Dr. Graham," one of the undergrad students said as we stepped inside the old, musty building.

"Hi Misty."

Grinning, Misty glanced at James, then smiled at me.

James walked right into the classroom with me and set my computer bag on the table that served as a desk.

At least a dozen students had already found seats in the new to them classroom and settled in. Misty sat down in one of the front row seats.

"I'll see you after class," James said.

"Okay," I said, as though it was the most normal thing in the world, even though I had absolutely no idea what he was thinking.

After he left, Misty leaned forward.

"He's cute," she said.

"Yes," I said, unable to hide a little smile. "He is, isn't he?"

I pulled out my computer and turned it on. Found a couple of dry erase markers in my bag.

"Is he your boyfriend?" Misty asked.

"What? No." The answer was a reflex. I didn't even think. I didn't tell her that he used to be.

"You should date him," Misty said.

"I don't know," I said. "I've known him a really long time."

"So? He likes you."

I didn't respond. I didn't have a response.

But as I checked attendance, I couldn't help thinking about her words.

I didn't know if she was right or not.

But I did know that I liked him.

Something so simple and unexpected as having him show up to walk me to class brightened my day and had me feeling that giddiness of a college student all over again.

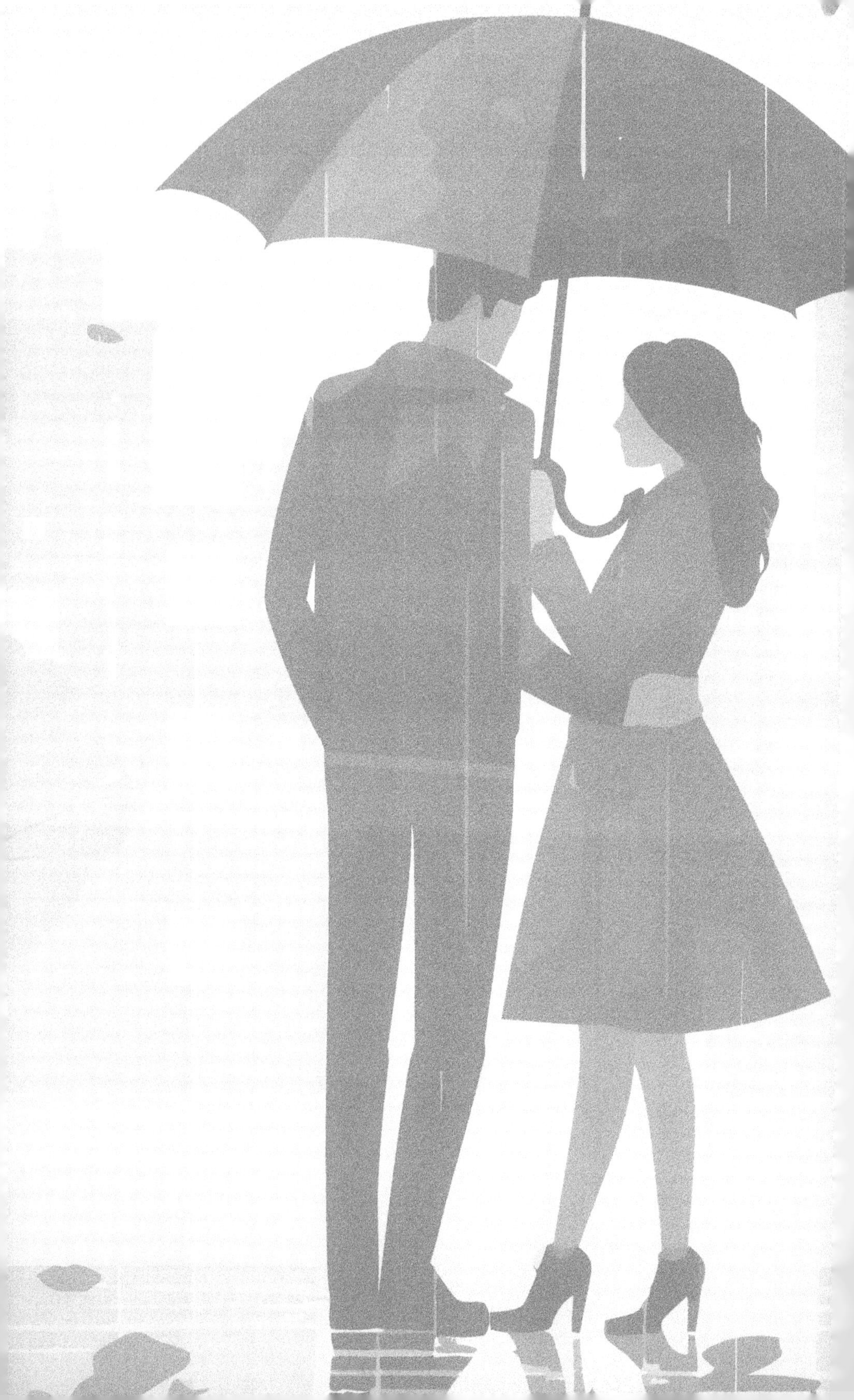

Chapter Ten

JAMES

I'd been busy all week with flights. I'd had to make three flights over to Philadelphia, a flight over to Chicago, and an overnight up to Mackinac Island.

Mackinac Island was by far one of my favorite places and having an overnight there made it even better. Definitely not a hardship.

It was a beautiful time of year. The island hadn't been open long to tourists and it still had a fresh, clean feel about it.

While I was there, I'd walked along the beach and I had thought about Tori.

I was going to see her again. And soon.

The way I saw it, we were starting over.

We couldn't just pick up where we had left off. Too many years had passed under the bridge.

We were the same, but different.

Fifteen years was a long time.

Things happened and people changed.

I believed that at the core she and I were the same people and we would get back to where we had been, but it would take some work to get us there.

I could tell she was wary.

If I was a betting man, I'd put my money on the wedding ring. I'd seen her glance at my hand.

I blamed Daryl for that. If he hadn't been such an ass about the whole Tiffany thing, I would have done what any self-respecting man would do. I would have lost the wedding ring.

It had done more than keep Daryl from ribbing me, though. It had also kept the guys from trying to set me up with someone new. They always wanted to set up the newly divorced guy, even if his wedding had led to no more than a quick annulment.

I knew the rhythm of the university. I knew that Tori's class would last fifty minutes. Possibly even forty-five. Maybe, depending on student interaction, she could be there for an hour. That part I didn't have a feel for just yet.

So I wandered the campus and gauged my time to put me back at her door at ten forty-five.

She wouldn't be expecting me.

Surprising her was half the fun. The funny thing about it was I didn't know if Tori liked surprises. I'd never really had the opportunity to surprise her when we had been dating.

We had just always been together. We'd known each other's schedules and, in fact, we had purposely coordinated them.

I'd had a double major in business and aviation while she

majored in psychology. We'd only actually had a couple of classes together.

Maybe I had taken her for granted. Maybe that was why we had drifted apart. Maybe I had always thought we would end up back together, so I hadn't put in the required effort. I'd just sort of let things happen.

It had been three years after she moved to Salt Lake City before I went on a date.

That's how much of a hold she'd had on me.

I didn't want anyone else.

I never had and I never would.

I'd proven to myself that I could move on if I had to, but truly, why would I?

I just had to make sure I got her on board.

Standing outside her classroom again, I listened to her interact with her students. I even recognized the topic.

Positive and negative reinforcement. Positive and negative punishment.

Not easy concepts to grasp, but if anyone could figure out how to convey the differences, it would be Tori.

Her students liked her. I could tell. And she liked them.

She was most definitely doing what she should be doing. It was a good fit.

When she happened to glimpse me standing outside the door, she missed a beat.

I grinned.

It was nice to know that I still had that kind of effect on Dr. Victoria Graham.

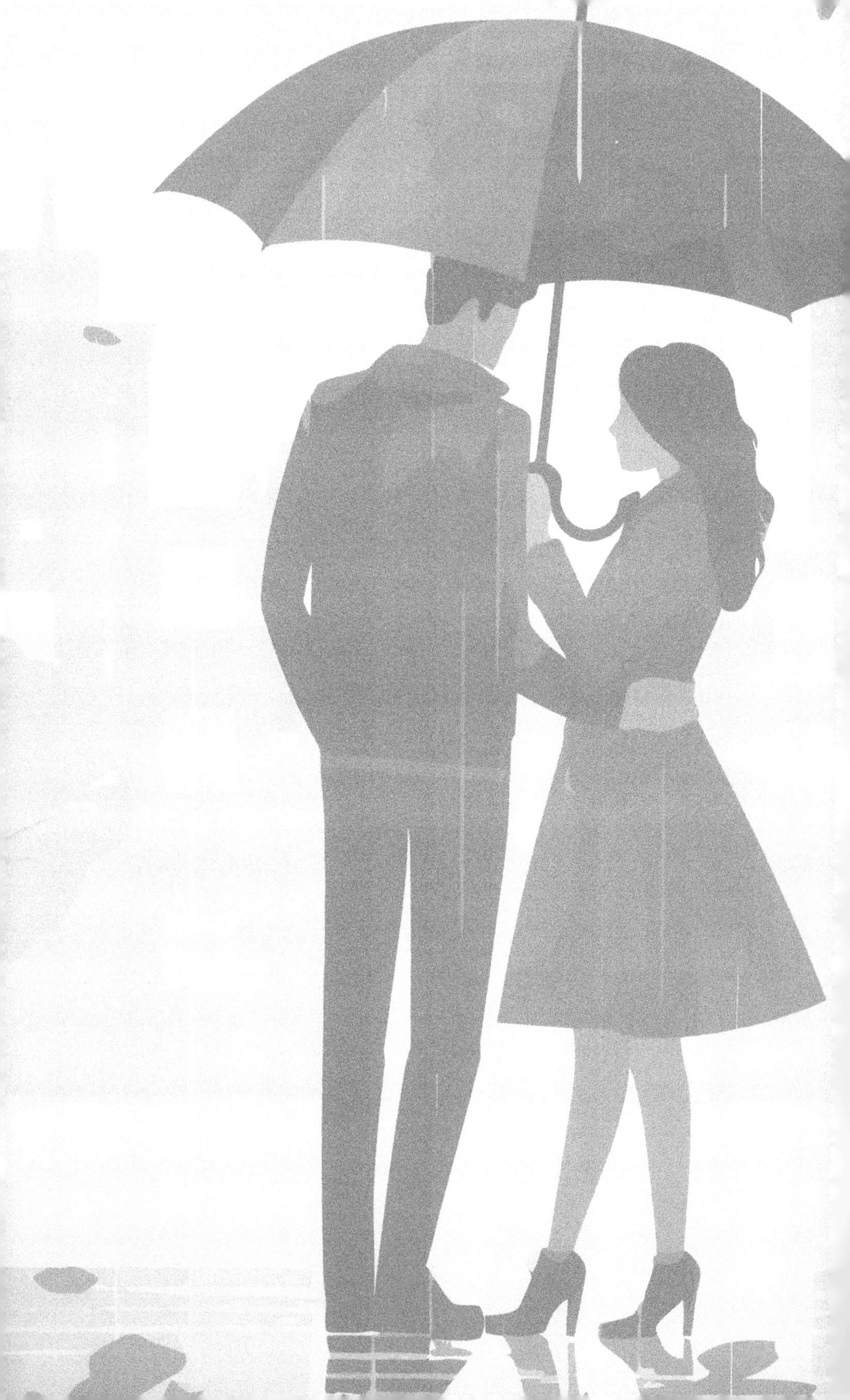

Chapter Eleven

VICTORIA

I was finishing up an explanation between positive and negative reinforcement when I caught a glimpse of James standing outside my door.

He stood across the hall, one foot propped behind him against the wall. He looked every bit like the self-assured, confident pilot that he was.

Apparently he had grown into the Ashton name. As a young adult, no one would have known he was an Ashton, the oldest son of one of the wealthiest families in Pittsburgh.

But now, it took no more than a glance to see that he exuded success. And not just the kind that came from being a successful private airplane pilot—not that that was nothing—but also the kind that came from old money.

Old money had a look.

Like him, I hadn't given it much thought when we had dated, but now I could see it. He exuded it. He was wearing jeans and a worn black leather jacket. But it wasn't his clothes or his two hundred dollar haircut. It was the way he held himself.

The confident expression on his face. The devil may care what anyone else thought attitude.

I caught all that in that simple quick glance.

If that wasn't enough to have me missing a beat, then the way he was watching me certainly was.

He was looking at me in that way. The way that told me he had not forgotten about how close we had been. That he just might want to be close like that again.

I answered a couple of other questions.

"Why do they call it negative reinforcement?" A young student name Mike asked.

"Remember," I said. "Don't think of positive and negative as good and bad. Think of positive as adding and negative as taking something away.

"If you add something. Do something. And behavior increases then it is positive reinforcement.

"If you subtract something. Stop doing something. And behavior increases, then it is still reinforcement, but it is negative reinforcement. Does that make sense?"

"Sort of," he said.

Milly piped in. "It's like the seatbelt, right?"

"Yes," I said. "Imagine your car has an annoying alarm that beeps if you don't fasten your seatbelt."

The students laughed.

"The beeping sound is an aversive stimulus. The behavior that is strengthened is fastening the seatbelt. When you fasten your seatbelt, the beeping stops, removing the aversive stimulus. This encourages you to continue fastening your seatbelt in the future to avoid the annoying beeping.

"Negative reinforcement."

I took a breath and pointed to the chart I'd drawn on the board. "Remember, look at the behavior first. Did it go up or down."

The alarm on my phone went off, signaling the end of class.

"Think about it," I said. "Try to come with your own examples. If you have questions I'll answer them on Wednesday."

Then there was the loud chaos of students packing up to leave class.

My hands shook a little as I packed up my own computer.

James.

James did that to me.

He'd always had an effect on me. But now, seeing him after all these years, brought a whirlwind of feelings crashing over me.

It was one thing having him just so happen to be the one to rescue me from the building.

It was another thing entirely to have him waiting for me outside my classroom door. The same way he had waited for me after class a million times when we were college students.

Slinging my leather computer bag over my shoulder, I walked out of the now empty classroom toward James.

He pushed off the wall and took my computer bag from me without asking.

"Want to have lunch at that new hamburger place?"

"Sure," I said, pushing my hair back and walking with him down the hallway.

How did he do this? How did he just swoop back into my life without a hitch? Like all those years had just folded up on themselves and vanished.

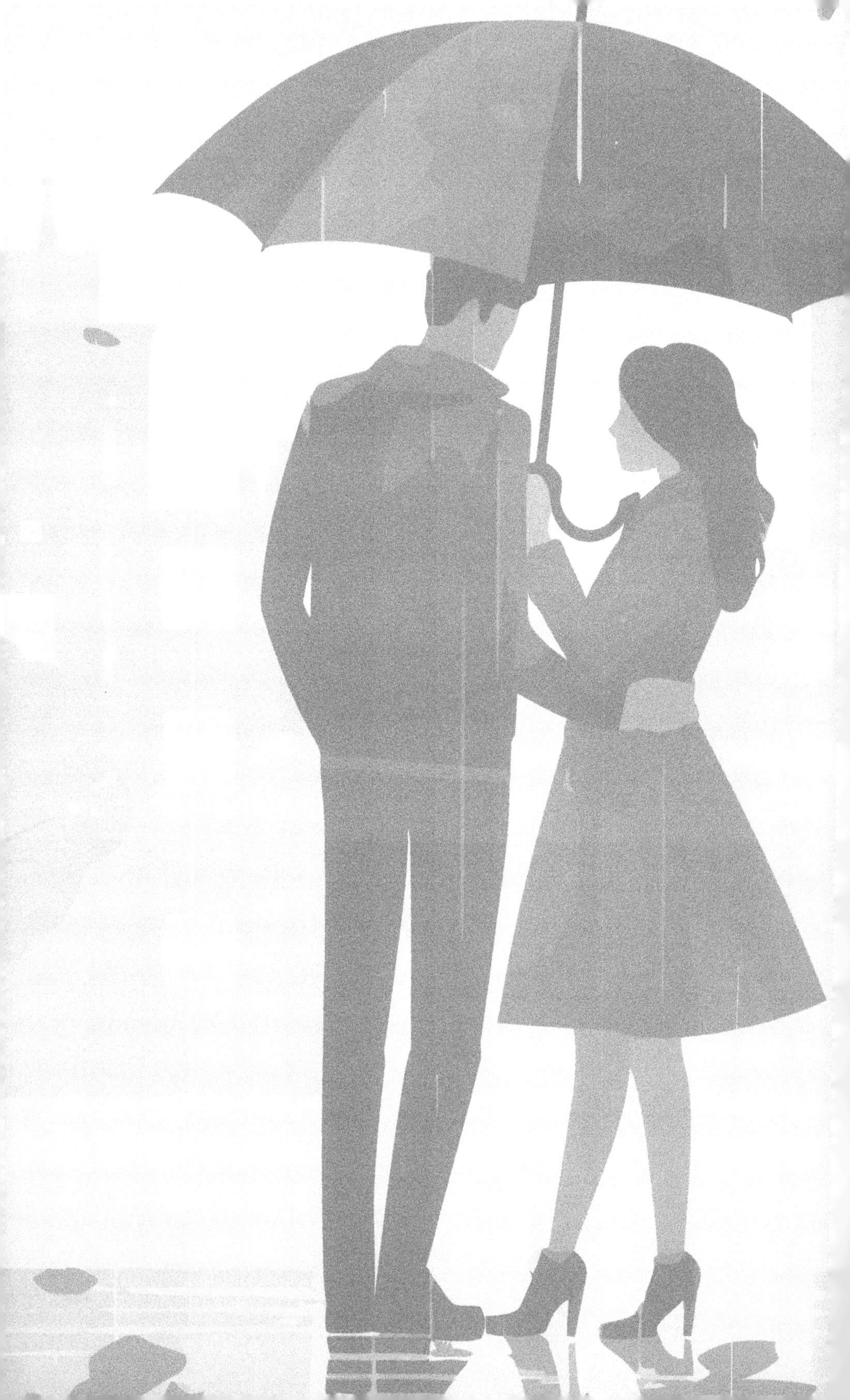

Chapter Twelve

JAMES

I didn't have a plan. Not exactly anyway.

Tori and I walked across campus toward where I had left my truck parked in a visitor's parking spot.

The air was about right for early October. The sun was bright, but the breeze was cool. Chilly even.

Tori wasn't wearing a jacket. Just black slacks and a white long sleeve shirt. The white canvas sneakers were a cute touch. She had many facets and one of them was a practical side. The shoes came from her practical side.

Knowing she had to be cold, about halfway to my truck, I stopped and shrugged out of my jacket, then placed it over her shoulders.

"Thanks," she said, sliding her arms into the sleeves. The jacket swallowed her, the arms hanging over her hands.

"You're welcome."

"It was supposed to be warmer today."

"I know," I said. "My truck is right up here."

"You were just in the neighborhood?" she asked.

"Something like that."

"It seems you keep coming to my rescue."

"It's what I do best."

I opened the door and gave her a boost inside before going around to my side of the truck.

"How is your car?" I asked.

"Unscathed. I stopped by the dealership to make sure I wasn't missing anything. They said it was fine."

"Good."

I turned onto the highway.

"I heard you in class. You're good at what you do."

"I like it," she said with a little shrug.

"It shows," I said. "You teach graduate students, too."

"How did you know that?"

"I had to ask around to find you," I said. "But it's on the Internet."

"Right. Of course. Everything is on the Internet." She grinned over at me.

Her smile nearly took my breath away.

It was her eyes. Green eyes like a deep lush forest that glowed like sunlight flickering through the leaves when she smiled.

She had my heart. Always had.

My attention shifted as I pulled onto the freeway, heading toward next exit where the restaurant was.

She pushed at the sleeves on my leather jacket, shoving them up enough to check her phone.

"Everything okay?" I asked.

"Yeah. I made the mistake of telling my mother about the tree falling on my building. Now she's suddenly worried about me."

"Kind of after the fact, right?"

"I know. It's weird, isn't it?"

I took the next exit, made the first right. I remembered that her parents worked all the time, not having much time for Tori. Not as bad as Tiffany's family, but still nothing like the closeness of my family.

"There's no explaining parents."

"How are yours? And your grandparents?"

"They're great. You should come to dinner on Sunday."

Even as I parked in front of the restaurant, I didn't miss the widening of her eyes.

"I think maybe there's something we need to talk about first," she said.

My gut clenched. It was time to explain why I'd been wearing a wedding ring and why I wasn't wearing it now.

I didn't want to talk about Tiffany. I really didn't even want Tori to know about her, but it couldn't be helped. I'd never kept things from Tori. Now was not the time to start.

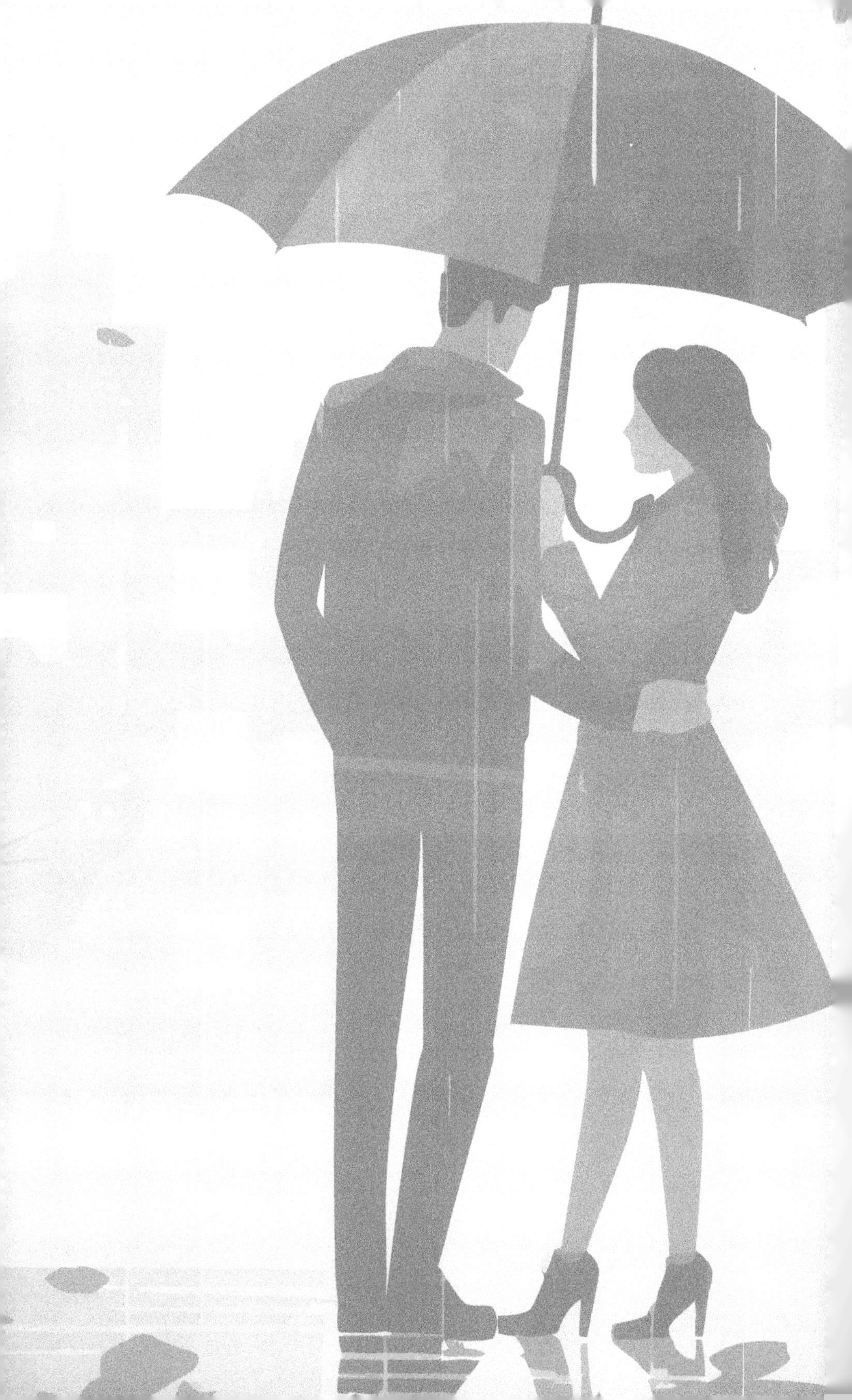

Chapter Thirteen

Victoria

James came around and opened the passenger door. Although he was there, he kept his hands to himself as I slid out of the truck.

He looked a bit troubled.

I'd brought up something he didn't want to talk about.

I knew him too well not to know.

The hostess, a college student I'd seen around on campus, but didn't know, seated us at a table near the window. Even though the little square table had four chairs, we sat next to each other so we could both look outside.

"Your server will be right with you, Mr. Ashton," she said.

"Thanks," James said with a little wince.

"You know her," I said.

"Not really. I was here with Bella last week. They know each other and she introduced me."

"She remembered you." I slipped out of his leather jacket and laid it carefully across the back of the chair between us.

How could the girl not remember James? To her he would be an older man, but that didn't take away from his charming handsomeness.

"She called me Sir," he said, leaning close.

I laughed and admittedly felt a little relieved.

For a minute I'd worried that the older version of James was flirty with younger girls. Obviously I'd been hanging out with the wrong kind of guys.

I shook off the feeling and picked up the menu.

"What's good here?" I asked.

Even though I was the one who had brought it up, I was putting off talking to him about his wedding ring.

A part of me… a big part of me… kind of didn't want to know.

I preferred to imagine him spending the last fifteen years working and not dating, much less getting married.

I was being a chicken.

"I like the chicken salad," he said.

I looked up sharply at him.

"You still eat chicken, right?"

"Yes," I said. "I was just thinking about chicken."

"We're on the same wavelength then." He set his menu aside.

"Right. Chicken salad sounds good." I closed my menu, set it aside, and took a deep breath.

"You wanted to talk to me about something," he said.

I'd secretly hoped he'd forgotten or that he at least wouldn't bring it up again.

I was a psychologist. Psychologists knew that communication was the key to everything.

"Are you in a relationship?" I asked, jumping right in and getting to the point.

"No." He said it quickly and sat back.

I nodded. Considered. Just get it over with.

"I thought I saw a ring."

"You did." He ran a hand through his hair. "It's a long story."

"I'm not going anywhere."

"Of course you aren't."

It was odd, but I took heart that talking about this made him a little uncomfortable. I couldn't explain why. Maybe because it meant he cared what I thought.

"I dated a girl for a while. A few months. Getting married seemed like the thing to do."

I nodded, keeping my expression blank. I forced myself to think of him just like any other client. Otherwise, if I let myself get emotionally involved, it would hurt too much.

"She didn't want a big wedding because she had a small family and I don't."

"I can see where that would be a concern."

He shot me a look.

"So I caved and we flew to Vegas. Had a quick ceremony. I started feeling uneasy on the flight out there. I chalked it up to wedding jitters."

"Cold feet."

"Yeah. Well. I forced my way through it. We got it annulled less than a month later."

"You just changed your mind?"

"I knew it wasn't right. Looking back, I knew it all along."

"It just felt like the thing to do," I said, reflecting his words back.

"It did. I kept telling myself I could do it."

"I don't understand. What do you mean you could do it?"

Before he could answer, the server came to take our order.

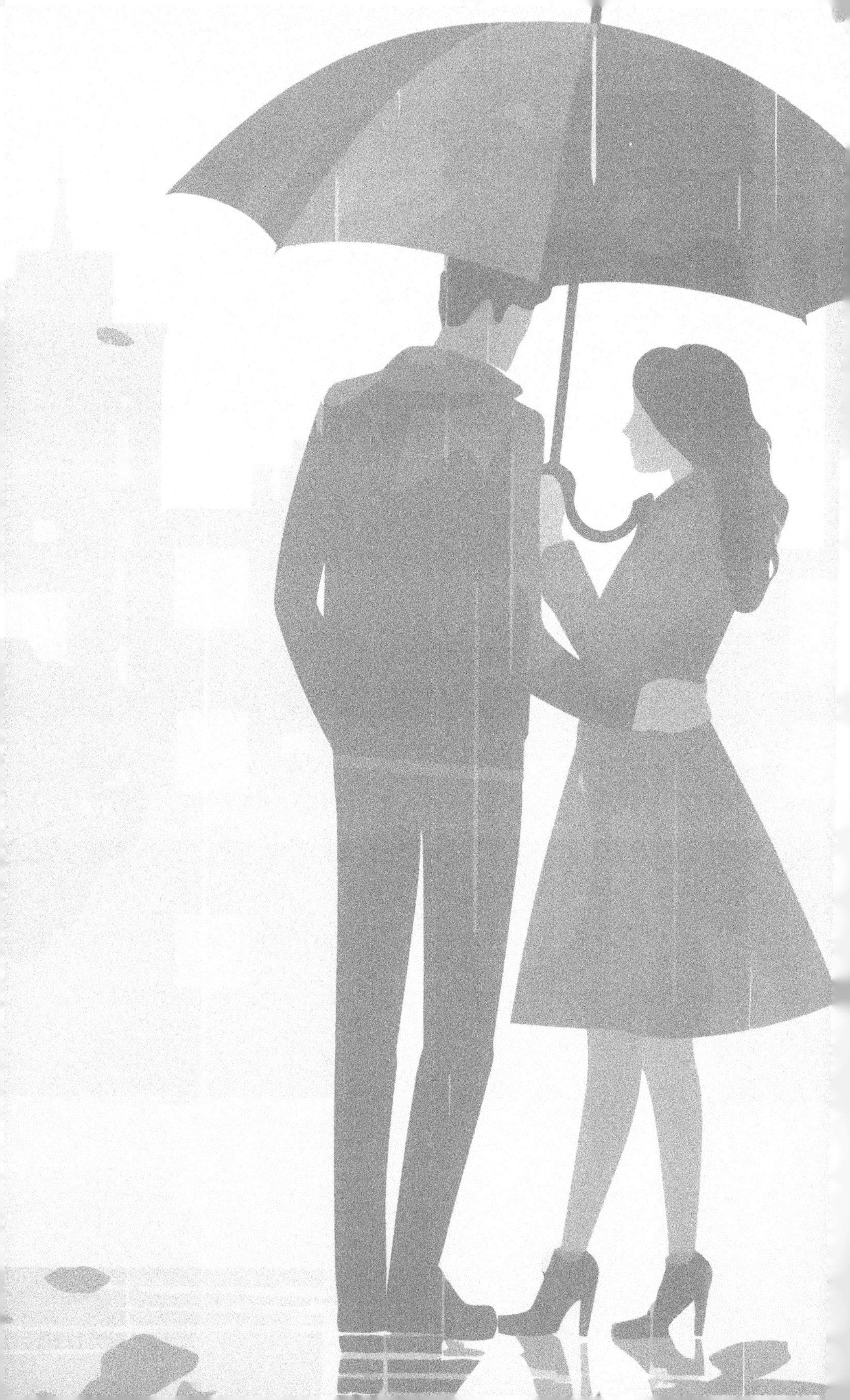

Chapter Fourteen

JAMES

The server, I think her name was Meghan or Mandy, brought our food and we ate in silence for a bit.

I hadn't meant to go in to that much detail about Tiffany and the wedding.

But Tori was good. She was a psychologist with lots of training in getting people to talk.

There was that and then, well, she was Tori and I could talk to her.

"James?" Tori asked, pulling me out of my thoughts. "How long ago was the annulment?"

"Early summer," I said.

"But the ring. You were still wearing the ring."

"One of the firemen, a guy named Daryl, told me I was making a mistake from the word go. I didn't want to admit to him that he was right. It was easier to just wear the ring."

Tori smiled a slow smile.

"Thanks for telling me this."

"I could always tell you anything. Right?"

"Right."

"I didn't want to tell you."

"Why not?" She picked up her glass and sipped her coke.

"It's not something I'm proud of."

"I think it's called life."

I blew out a breath. I'd known she would be understanding.

"Okay. I told you mine. You tell me yours."

She looked blankly at me. I could see her thinking.

"I don't have anything," she said.

"You have to have something. You can't have gone this far in life and not have something."

"I think." She took a deep breath. Let it out. "I think not having anything is my something."

"It's okay," I said. "Tell me about Salt Lake City."

I knew how hard it had been for me to tell her about Tiffany. I wouldn't have told her yet, but I'd backed myself into a corner by wearing my wedding ring in front of her. Which, by the way, was in a box in my closet now.

I didn't care what Daryl had to say. I wasn't going to get myself in a bind like that again.

Her face brightened.

"Salt Lake was good. I really liked it."

"Working at the mental hospital?"

"It felt like I was in the trenches. I worked with people who had hit rock bottom. They didn't have anywhere to go but up. I could literally see their improvement almost from the time they got there."

"But you didn't want to keep doing it?"

"Part of me did," she said. "Maybe a big part. But my heart was with teaching. And now I get to train graduate students so they can go out there and help people. It feels like the best of both worlds."

"Either way," I said. "You're good at it."

"I like it."

"And modest."

The server laid our ticket on the table and I handed her my credit card.

"So now that you have an explanation for my transient marital status, are you coming to my family's Sunday dinner with me?"

"I'm not so sure that's a good idea."

I'd told her too much.

"I shouldn't have told you all that," I said.

"That's not it."

She had a boyfriend. That had to be it.

A girl like Tori would have a boyfriend. He might not live in Pittsburgh, but she would have a boyfriend.

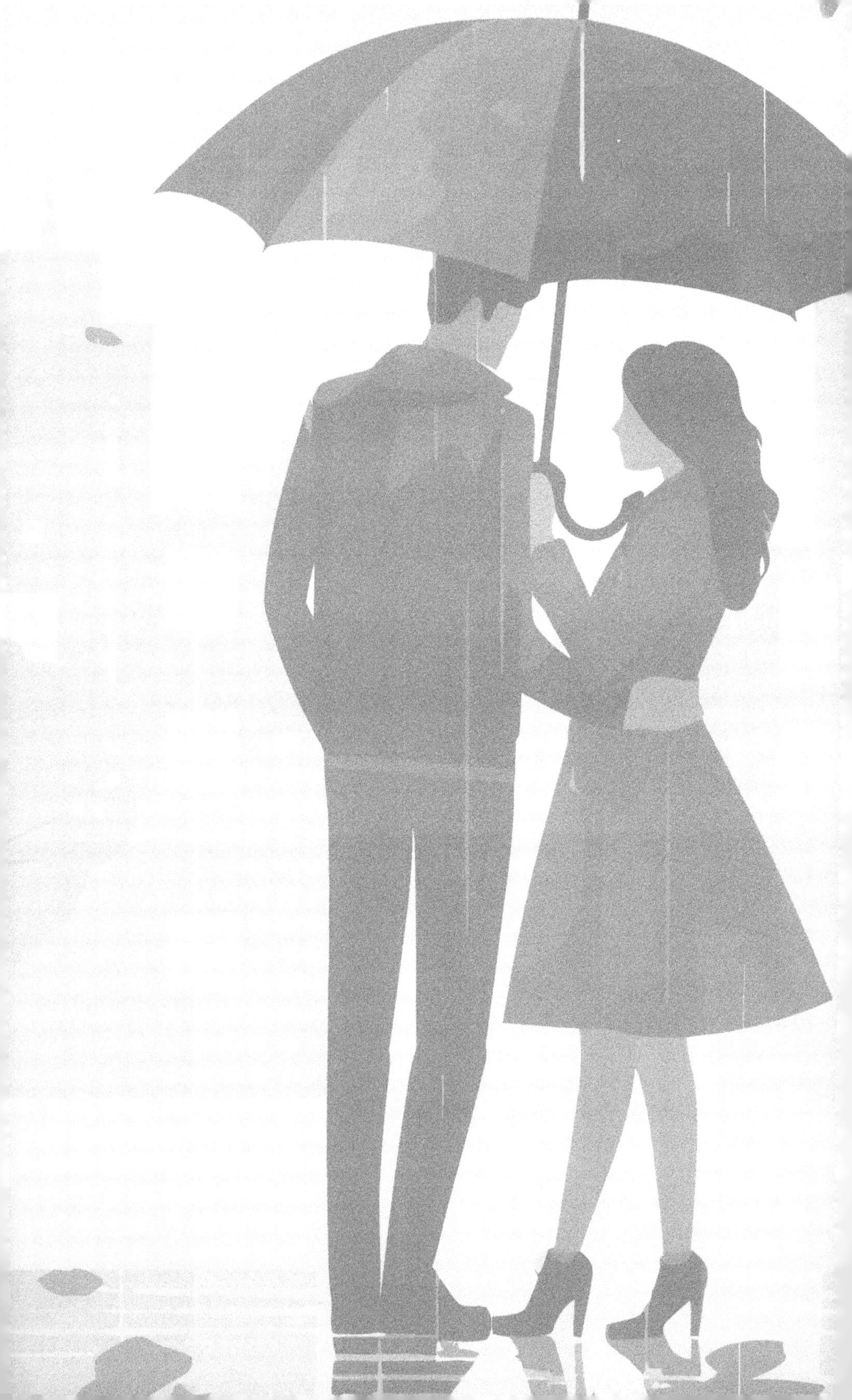

Chapter Fifteen

VICTORIA

When we stepped outside, the fresh air cooled my skin.

I would not be surprised to see a late season snowfall this year. The weather felt right for it. Cloudy with a nip in the air.

"Is that new?" James asked looking toward a little park across the street.

It used to be just a railroad track, but now they had cleared away the underbrush and turned the unused area into a park.

"It looks new," I said.

"Let's check it out," he said, grabbing my hand and leading me across the street.

The park was definitely new. There was a set of adult-sized swings and half a dozen benches scattered around a little firmly packed dirt path.

"Is it open?" I asked. "There's no one here."

"It looks open to me," he said, not missing a step. "How long has it been since you were in a swing?"

Since the last time you and I went to a park.

"I don't know," I said. "A while."

"You sit," he said. "I'll push."

I sat in the swing grasped the steel chains.

"You ready?" he asked.

"Why not?" I asked, moving my feet on the ground just enough to get the swing moving.

James gave me a little push and my feet left the ground.

"You can swing, too."

"I'd rather push you," he said.

Grown up James wasn't so different from younger James. Younger James had been unselfish and giving.

Grown up James, it seemed, was also unselfish and giving.

He wanted to me go with him to his family's house on Sunday.

It was probably no big deal to him. Just another Sunday afternoon with his family.

I tried to imagine his brothers and sisters all grown up. My brain couldn't quite go there. In my head, they were forever young. Just like James had been until I saw him again last week.

Now that I'd spent some time with him, I didn't notice that he was older. I looked at him and saw the same person I had dated in college.

But he wasn't the same person.

He'd been married. Divorced, but still. He'd been married.

I hadn't been married. I had barely dated.

I'd put my head down and focused on graduate school. Then work.

James pushed the swing and I went high, the wind sweeping through my hair.

I was afraid.

Not of the swing. Swings didn't scare me.

James scared me.

I was afraid that if he pulled me back into his world, I wouldn't want to leave.

And even that wasn't what really scared me. What really scared me was that he wouldn't feel the same way.

He had obviously moved on. He'd moved on when I couldn't. Or maybe more accurately, I didn't want to.

I'd had ample opportunities. I'd even had two marriage proposals. Both of them were from men I barely knew and hadn't even dated. Apparently they had thought I was marriage material.

I didn't disagree, but I wasn't going to marry someone I wasn't in love with.

There had only been one man I'd ever been in love with.

That man was currently pushing my swing, sending me high into the sky, sending my heart racing.

It wasn't just the swing. It was James.

James had always sent my blood racing.

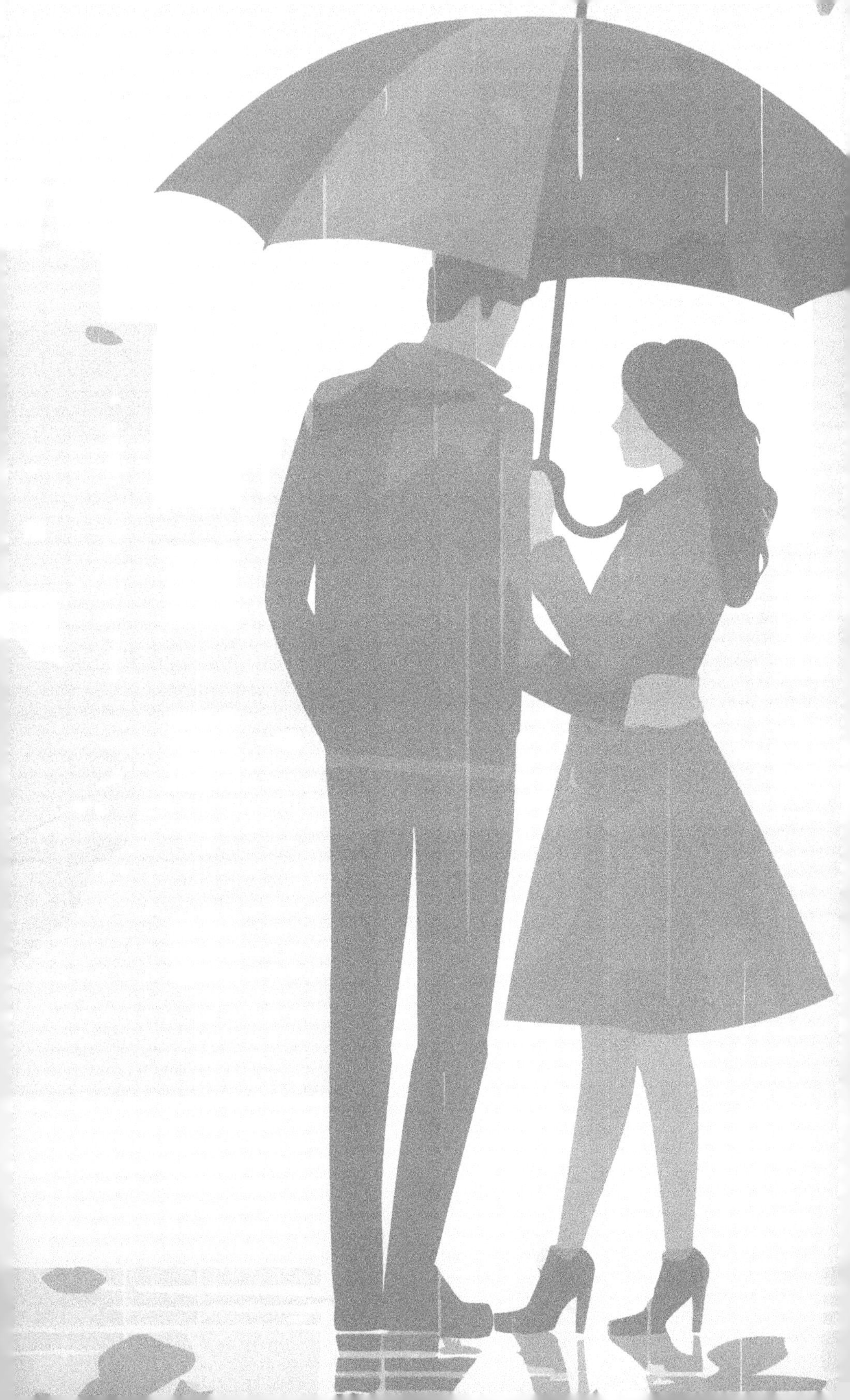

Chapter Sixteen

JAMES

Tori looked better as we walked back toward my truck. Her cheeks were flushed with color, making her even more beautiful as if that was possible.

Her eyes were bright as she watched me climb into the driver's seat.

"I guess I should have asked if you had an afternoon class."

"Fortunately I don't," she said, glancing at her watch. "I did have office hours which I missed."

"Oh. Sorry."

"It's okay. No one knows where to find me right now with our offices all moved around."

"I like the way you think," I said, backing out onto the road.

"I'm not the best role model right now."

"Everybody deserves to have a little bit of fun now and then."

"You're right." She smiled.

"Just stick with me, kid."

"You're trouble," she said.

I went the back route this time, avoiding the freeway. I didn't have a logical reason. Maybe it was just because it would take a little longer to get back with the stop signs and traffic lights to contend with.

I wasn't ready to let her go yet.

A flight request had come in while we were at lunch, though, so I needed to get to the airport.

A bit of a double standard perhaps. Me keeping her from her office hours while I made sure I made my flight.

"If anybody gives you a hard time about your office hours," I said. "Just tell them I kidnapped you."

"Right. Like they're going to believe that."

"It is a full moon."

She looked at me sideways.

"It's the middle of the day."

I just raised an eyebrow in response.

"Never mind. You would know that," she said.

Pilots had to be part meteorologists. It just so happened that I had always been a student of the weather.

"Since you won't go to Sunday dinner with me, which I don't blame you, by the way. My family is a little crazy."

"I can only imagine that things have gotten especially kinda crazy since you found out about your grandfather changing his name and being Noah Worthington's brother."

"I admit that it did change some of the family dynamics."

"In a good way?"

"I think so. We see Noah and his wife Savannah on holidays now."

"They have a big family?"

"Oh my Heavens. You wouldn't believe," I said. "Where do you need me to drop you?"

"You can park in visitors and I can walk."

I pulled into a visitors spot.

"Our family is tiny compared to the Worthingtons."

"I can't even imagine." She put her hand on the door knob.

"Wait," I said. "I'll come around."

She waited, but I could tell she was ready to go.

I opened the door and she slid out.

"Thanks for lunch," she said, taking a step backwards. "See you later." Then she took off down the sidewalk headed back toward her office.

Even though I didn't want to, I let her go. I couldn't just follow her around everywhere like a puppy.

Besides, I had a flight.

As I climbed back in my truck, I realized that I hadn't gotten the chance to ask her to go flying with me.

I'd been about to ask her, but we'd started talking about my family.

Tori was like that. Good at keeping the conversation away from herself. She'd always been good at it, but now that she was a trained psychologist, she was even better at not talking about herself and getting others, namely me, to talk about myself.

I wasn't giving up though.

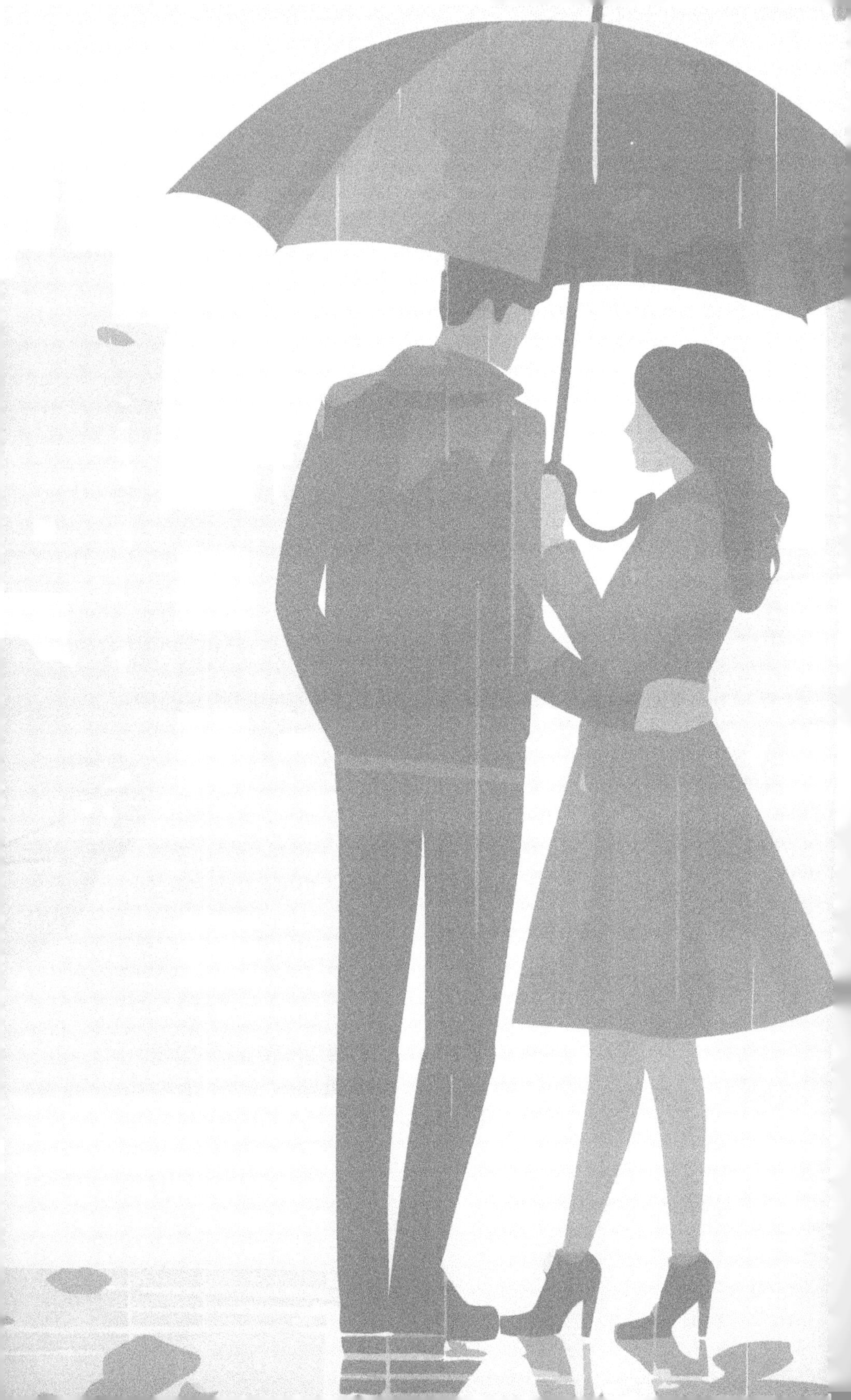

Chapter Seventeen

VICTORIA

No one seemed to notice that I had been absent for my office hours.

The disruption of having our building condemned and our offices subsequently scattered across campus made it hard to track anyone in particular.

Someone would have had a specific reason to come looking for me and even as far as anyone knew, I could be walking to the main office which was in an entirely different building on the other side of campus.

It was a mess and it promised to be a mess for the foreseeable future.

No one knew what they were going to do about our building. No one knew at this point if they were going to build a new building or if they were going to try to rearrange some of the other departments to give us our own space.

Either way it was going to be disruptive. It took years to have a new building approved and then years to build it.

Something like that didn't happen overnight.

They would figure something out. Our university had more psychology majors than any other majors. We might not get the shiny new modern building, but we pulled in a lot of students.

I sat at my desk—a makeshift oversized metal thing from the last century—powered on my computer, and got to work. I had a test to finish making for my developmental class on Thursday.

Just a few tweaks and it would be finished. That was one good thing about teaching the same classes year after year. A few minor updates here and there. Keep up with the latest literature, add it into the lectures, add and modify a couple of test questions, and everything was up to date.

It was, however, time to change textbooks in personality psych. Either keep the old text and adopt the new edition or find a new one. Since the last textbook had been chosen by someone else, I was inclined to at least see what new texts were out there.

As I worked, my thoughts kept wandering to James.

The more they wandered, the more I wrangled them back to the task at hand.

It was just as easy to choose a new text, maybe easier, than adapting a new edition.

Either way, I wasn't afraid of work. I enjoyed lecture prep. I enjoyed lecturing even more.

To enjoy standing in front of a group of students so much, I was a chicken when it came to James's family.

It was silly. I knew them. They would welcome me with open arms. At least I liked to think they would.

I didn't know what it was like with his ex-wife. Did they like her?

I closed the lid on my computer.

Ex-wife.

I ran a hand through my hair.

It was so strange thinking about James having an ex-wife.

But it had been annulled. It hadn't lasted.

Were they upset about it? Happy? Ambivalent?

It didn't matter.

If I saw him again. If he asked me again. I would go.

I would be brave.

And I would be true to my heart.

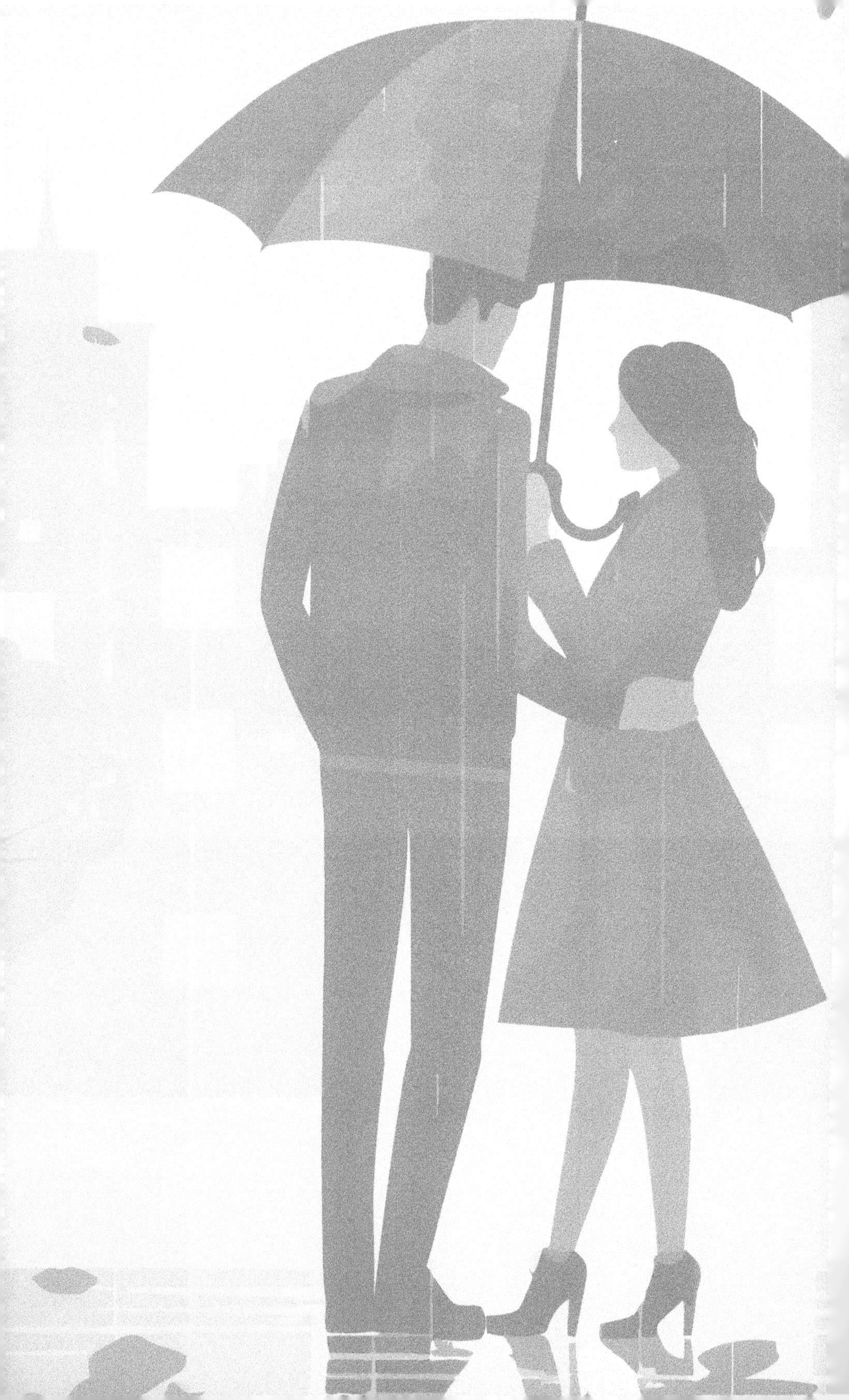

Chapter Eighteen

JAMES

After a quick flight over to Pittsburgh, I got home before sunset.

My sister Bella was leaning over the kitchen table, blueprints spread out all across the table.

"Hey," she said, looking up.

"Hey." I went straight to the refrigerator. Grabbed a coke. Went back to see what she was working on while I opened it.

"What are you working on?"

She straightened. "Something for Mrs. Bryan."

"It looks like a house."

"It is a house. Sort of. Actually it's a little office space for her. She's a writer, you know."

"Where is she putting it?"

"In her backyard."

"It's mostly windows, but..." I walked around the table looking. "It's got two floors."

I looked up at Bella.

"Bathroom and storage on second floor."

"Built in exercise." She put a hand on one hip and grinned. "It's actually pretty efficient."

"Brilliant."

"Thanks." She tapped me on the arm. "What are you so happy about?"

"I'm not happy about anything," I said.

She looked at me sideways.

"It's a girl."

"Has anyone ever told you that you're scary sometimes?"

She shrugged and sat down.

"It's not Tiffany," she said, picking up her pencil. "You never had that look with her. In fact you haven't had that look since..." She looked up at me. Squinted. "You saw Tori."

"Now you are REALLY scaring me."

"Sit," she pushed the nearest chair back with her foot. "Tell."

I sat down and I told her.

"She's still pretty, isn't she?"

"Of course."

"I knew she would be. You have to bring her over Sunday."

I shook my head. "Already asked. She won't do it."

"Why?"

"I don't know."

Bella stared blankly at her blueprints for a minute. "Built in bookcase here," she said, then looked up at me.

"Please tell me you didn't tell her about Tiffany."

"I told her," I said.

"That's why she won't come," Bella said.

"That's not a good reason."

"It's a very good reason," she said, with a quick glance around. "Everything is all messy now."

"It's not messy," I said with a halfhearted laugh.

"You moved on and she doesn't know what to expect."

"Okay, then. How do I fix it?"

At ten years younger than me, my sister Bella was one of the smartest people I knew.

"Okay," she said. "I think I know what you should do."

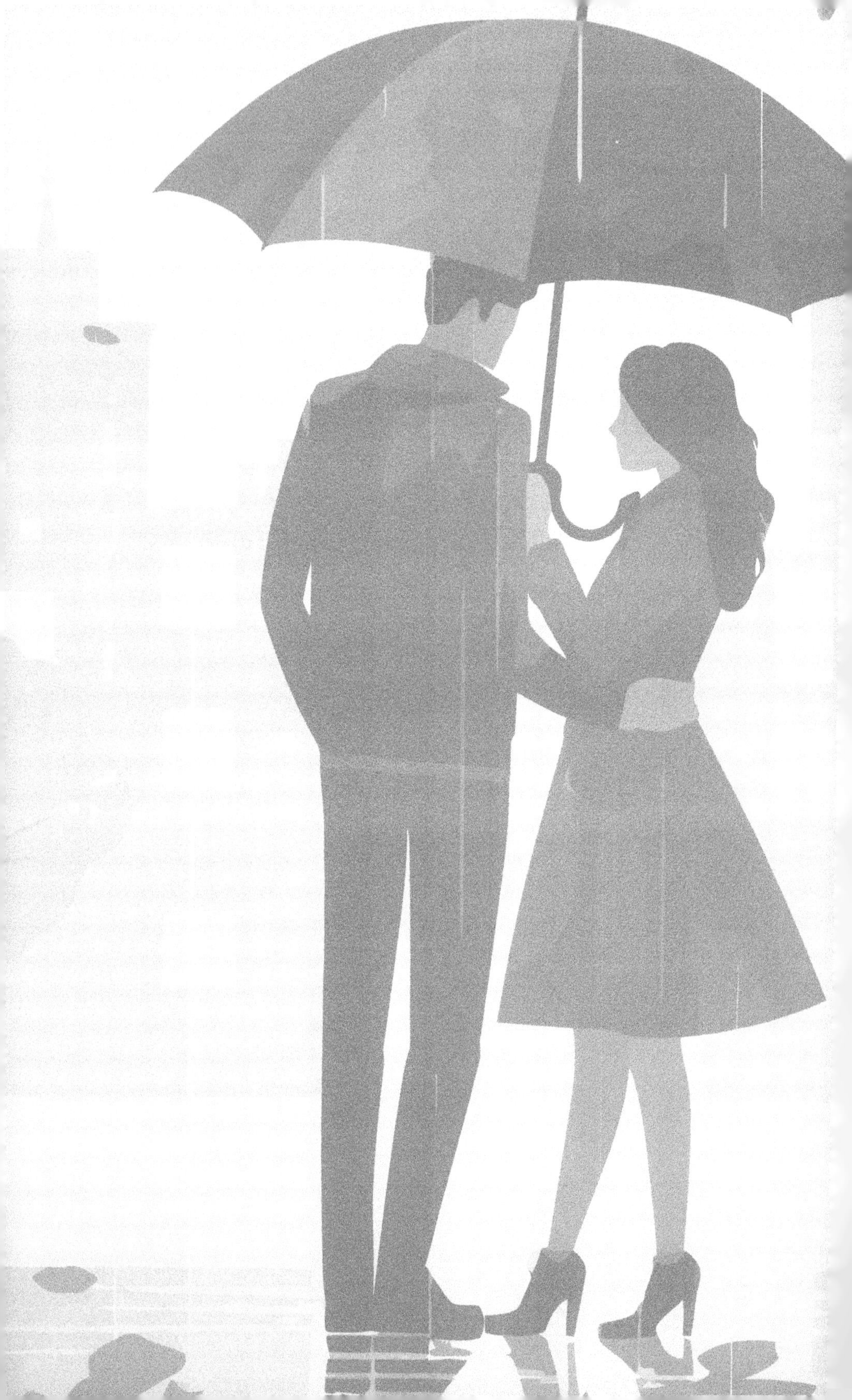

Chapter Nineteen

VICTORIA

I packed up my computer, left the office, and stayed true to my routine. I went home.

If anyone thought the life of a college professor was exciting, they were terribly mistaken.

After dropping my computer bag off in my study, I headed to the bedroom to change into sweatpants and a t-shirt. My apartment on the sixth floor of a mid-rise had a clear view of the Monongahela River.

After changing, I turned on the tea kettle and stood at the window while I waited for the water to boil.

A riverboat, all lit up and filled with tourist for a dinner tour, slowly made its way along the river. The traffic on the bridges was backed up as always. I was thankful I was here and not out there.

A small jet passed by overhead, heading west.

Seeing a passing airplane always gave me a little burst of butterflies in my stomach.

It could be James up there.

My teakettle clicked off so I made some tea. Added some honey.

I usually went into my office to work a couple of hours in the evenings, but tonight I decided to sit on the sofa instead.

I picked up a romance novel I was halfway through and settled in to do some reading and relax with my tea.

I read for about half an hour and was thinking about making a second cup of tea when my phone chimed.

> **UNKNOWN NUMBER**
> Hi Tori. It's James. Is it too late for you to talk?

My heart pounding like crazy, I stared at the message.

> How did you get my number?

> **UNKNOWN NUMBER**
> You have the same number

Oh. Right.

I hadn't deleted his number, but I'd gotten several new phones over the years and numbers didn't always transfer.

> I got a new phone.

While I waited for him to respond, I created a new contact, saving his number.

JAMES

Me too. Bella found your phone number
in one of those old contact notebooks.

>   Wow. That's strange.

JAMES

This is Tori, right?

>   Yes

There was silence.

I got up. Made another cup of tea and settled back on the sofa.

JAMES

How do I know?

>   Ask me something only I would know.

Thought bubbles.

I breathed in the steam from the hot tea and waited.

JAMES

Where was our first date?

>   I don't think we had one.

JAMES

Where did we meet?

>   Student Union. School dance. August
>   23. Dessert table.

JAMES

That's specific. Your turn.

Okay. I could play this game.

> Where was our first kiss?

JAMES
Your backyard. In the gazebo.

> When?

JAMES
It was a chilly October evening. Saturday, I think.

> I think so, too.

The neighbor's door slammed and it was quiet again for a couple of minutes before their door opened again. They were taking their dog, a black lab, out for a walk.

JAMES
What are you doing?

> I am having a cup of hot tea and reading a book.

JAMES
Psychology book?

> Romance novel

JAMES
Bella just drew up a blueprint for an office for our neighbor. She writes books. Romance, I think.

> Small world.

> Wait. Bella's an architect?

JAMES

Yes. Hard to believe.

I'm doing math in my head.

I sipped my tea and tried to imagine James's little sister all grown up. She was about fifteen years old when I last saw her.

JAMES

LOL. She's a college graduate. Works for a big firm, but wants to be on her own.

Has that Ashton entrepreneurial spirit.

JAMES

We all do. And now we know that we have Worthington blood.

Your grandfather and Noah have both been successful.

JAMES

I think Noah with Skye Travels wins.

No kidding

I'd read about Noah Worthington. He had started his own company, Skye Travels, with one little airplane and grew it into the most successful private airline company in the country. Although it was based in Houston, he had airplanes at various places from Mackinac Island to Whiskey Springs, Colorado and apparently now Pittsburgh.

I marked my place and set my book aside.

> Are you at your parents' house?

JAMES
> At the moment, yes.

I smiled to myself.

I would not be surprised if all the Ashton siblings lived at home with their parents. It wasn't odd.

Their house was too big for it to be odd.

It was more of a manor than a house, really.

We kept texting back and forth and when I looked up again, it was nearing Midnight.

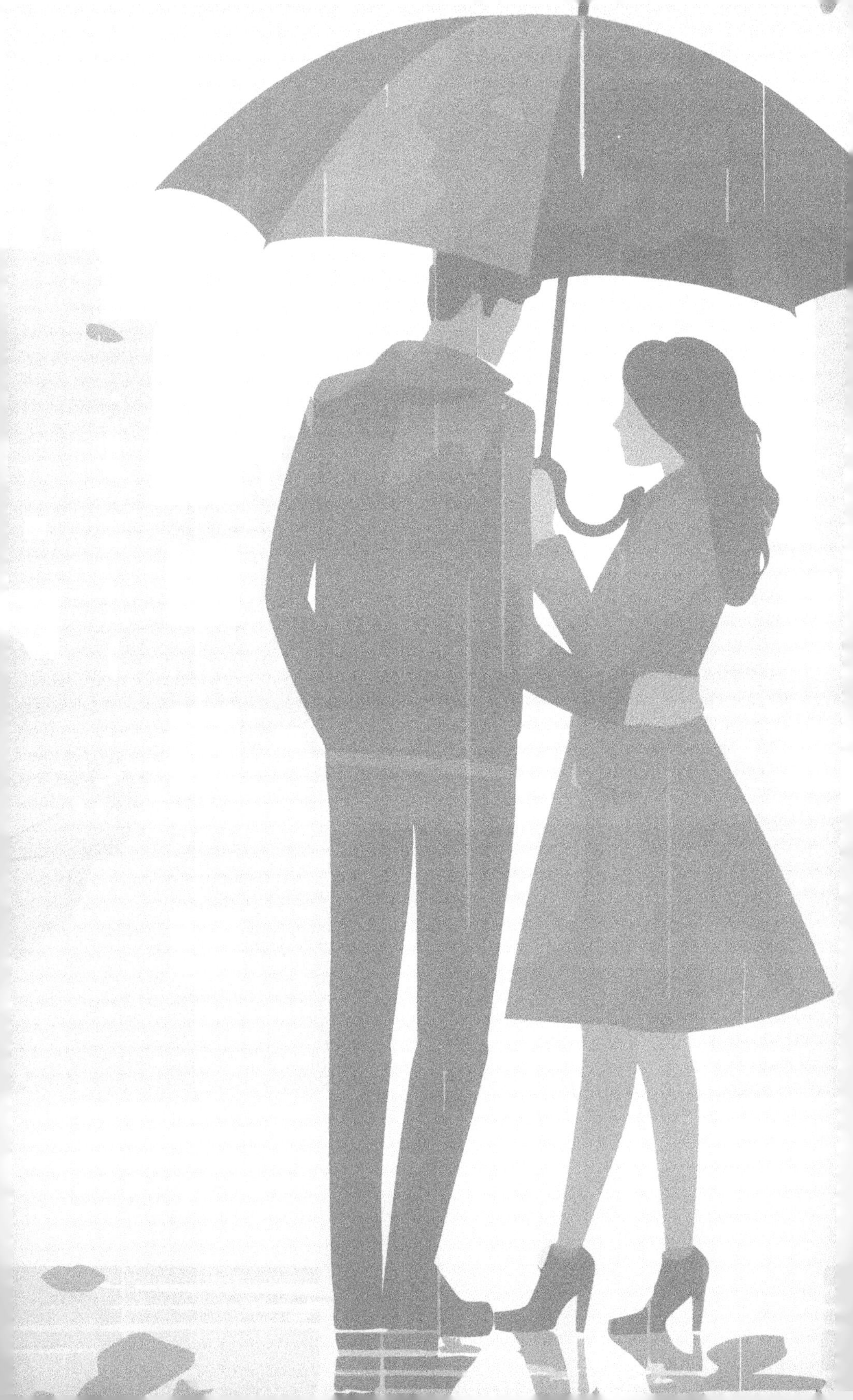

Chapter Twenty

JAMES

The next morning I showered and made it downstairs by seven o'clock for coffee.

Bella was there, dressed in her business attire, for work.

"How did it go?" she asked, handing me a cup of coffee, then making another for herself.

"You are brilliant," I said.

"I know."

"We texted back and forth for hours."

"See," she said, then checked her watch. "Now if I can just figure out how to get myself out of the corporate world."

"You'll figure it out."

"I know."

I tapped the blueprints, now neatly rolled up and stacked on the counter.

"This is a good start. More than."

"Maybe."

"You could sell these plans to other people."

"Like a template?"

"Exactly."

"I'll think about it." She put her cup in the dishwasher. "But right now I have to go. Fight traffic."

After Bella left, I sat down at the breakfast table and glanced at the newspaper. I was pretty sure we were one of the few people who still had an actual newspaper delivered to the door.

I liked it though. It was nice to hold something in my hands instead of just looking at a screen.

I flipped through and found a photograph of Woodard Hall being torn down. The article was titled "End of an Era."

They weren't kidding. Seeing it being scooped up like nothing more than debris put a knot in my stomach.

I made myself an egg and cheese sandwich, then hummed to myself as I cleaned up.

I had a dinner date with Tori tonight.

Bella really had found Tori's cell phone number in an old book of handwritten numbers.

Spending three hours texting about everything and nothing had done more to break the ice between us and reacquainting us than anything else would have.

Not only were we having dinner tonight, I was taking her flying on Saturday.

It was hard not to want to see her every day.

It would be so easy to fall back into the pattern of being attached at the hip like we had been fifteen years ago.

This time, however, I had to be more intentional with my actions.

This time I wanted her for keeps.

I'm not sure what it said, if anything, that my younger sister's idea about how to get Tori comfortable with me again worked.

At this rate, it wouldn't be long before I'd be bringing her home for Sunday dinner.

She'd agreed to go flying with me on Saturday.

For me that was just about as important as spending the day with my family.

Already, she knew that I was talking to my family, specifically Bella about her, and she knew that Bella had found her phone number.

I hadn't seen the need to tell her that it was still in my phone and even if it hadn't been in my phone, I had it memorized. 412-555-3534

The whole plan would have fallen apart if Tori had gotten a new phone number. Fortunately, people rarely did that anymore. Phone numbers were attached to everything. Almost as important as social security numbers.

Today I had to fly a businessman over to Chicago, then I'd be back in plenty of time to shower and get ready for my date.

It was going to be a good day.

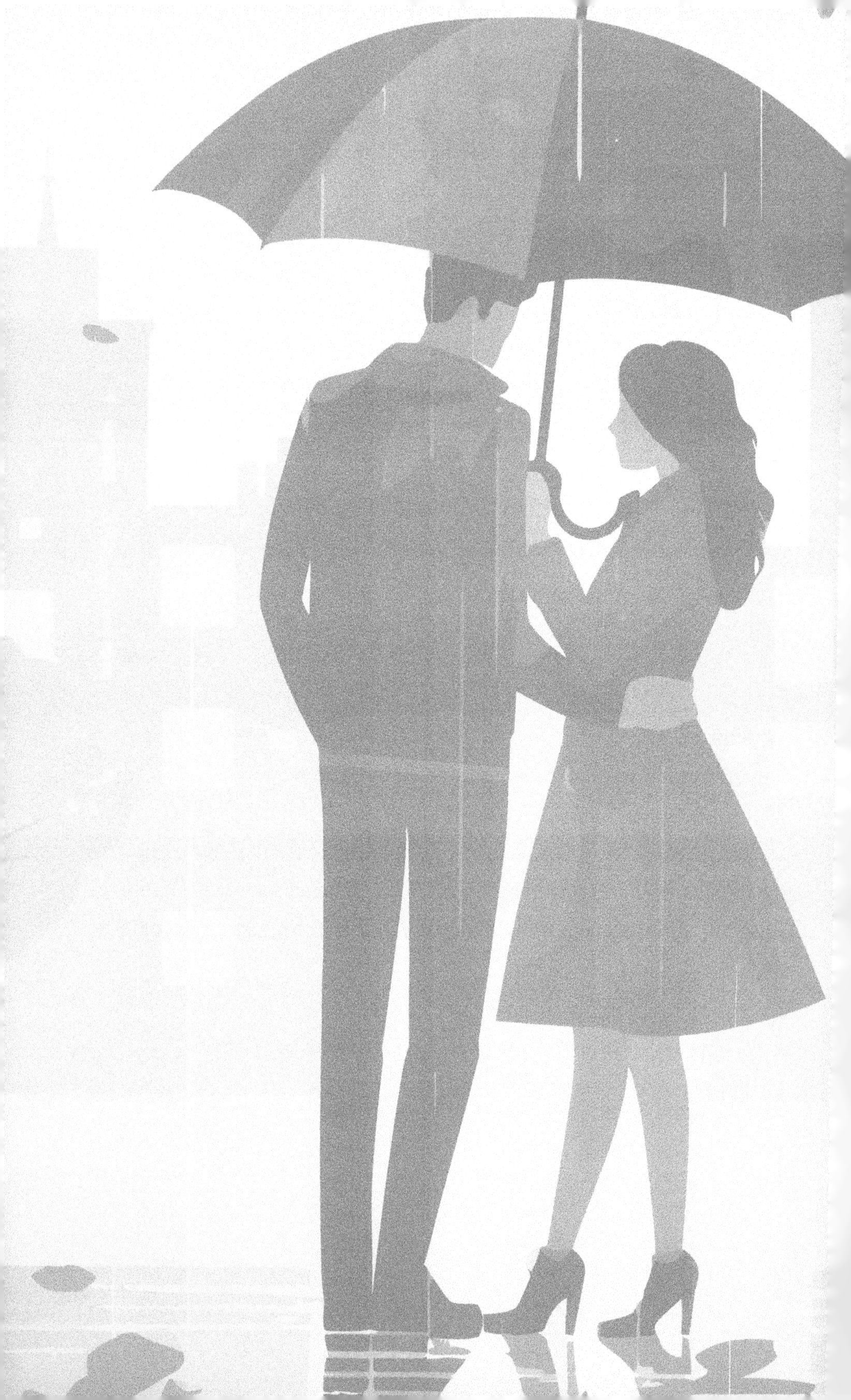

Chapter Twenty-One

VICTORIA

An unfortunate consequence of the psychology department losing their building was that our department chair decided that we needed more meetings. Instead of every other Friday, we were now having meetings every Friday and at random times like today.

The department chair, Dr. Angel Caldwell, was a very social person. If she had her way, our offices would all be in one big room so we could work and talk all day long.

The meetings were as unproductive as usual. The only thing different was the topic. Our building or lack thereof.

Seriously, you'd think the sky was falling and even worse, you'd think they could do something about it.

They wanted to get together after work for drinks. That was one thing I was going to avoid.

Besides. I had a date.

"Coming to the Pier tonight?" Dr. Mark Miller asked as we headed out. Mark and I had been hired at the same time. We'd bonded during orientation week.

"I don't think so," I said.

"Night class?"

"No. Just plans."

"You're braver than I am," he said, walking in step with me toward the elevator.

"How's that?"

"We're up for tenure next year."

"Right," I said, trying not to visibly shudder. The nightmares that circulated about the tenure process were not pretty.

"Trying to find a way to put that off."

Mark laughed as we stepped onto the elevator.

"Wait," he said. "You're serious."

"Sort of," I said, adding a smile to hopefully keep Mark from having a heart attack right here.

"I know what you mean," he said. "I've already started putting my materials together."

"How's fatherhood?" I asked, purposely changing the subject.

It worked, as expected. By the time we reached the end of the hall and went our separate ways, I'd gotten a play by play of three-month-old sleeping habits or rather lack thereof.

It was time for me to disappear to my office across campus. I would leave early and head home. I still didn't know what I was going to wear. It was just dinner. Something cute and casual. Maybe a dress. Something versatile since I didn't know where we were going.

I didn't think it would be casual pizza. We weren't college students anymore.

While I was walking across campus, I got a call from my mother.

"Hi Mom."

"Hi Tori. Do you have a class tonight?"

"I don't have a night class this semester."

"Oh good. Come over for dinner. Your father is going to make his spaghetti."

"I can't Mom. I have plans."

Students were in class right now, leaving the sidewalks deserted. I reached the little water fountain known as the Lady in the Mist and stopped to watch white birds swooping low, looking for insects.

"Plans to stay home by yourself? You really should get out more. You aren't getting any younger."

I removed the phone from my ear and glared at it.

"If you must know," I said, phone back to my ear. "I have a date."

"It's about time." She was silent a moment. "Bring him with you."

Not a chance."

"Can't," I said. "Raincheck."

What was it with people tonight?

First the department chair called an informal meeting at the Pier. Then my mother, whom I only talked to every week at the most, wanted me over for dinner.

All on the same night I had a date with James.

I looked up at the sky, to see if there was some kind of full moon, but, of course, daytime.

Maybe it was something in the air.

A nice autumn day.

My mother, though, had been acting differently since the tree fell on my building. It was sort of like she woke up and suddenly realized that anything could happen at any time.

She was too late though.

I had plans.

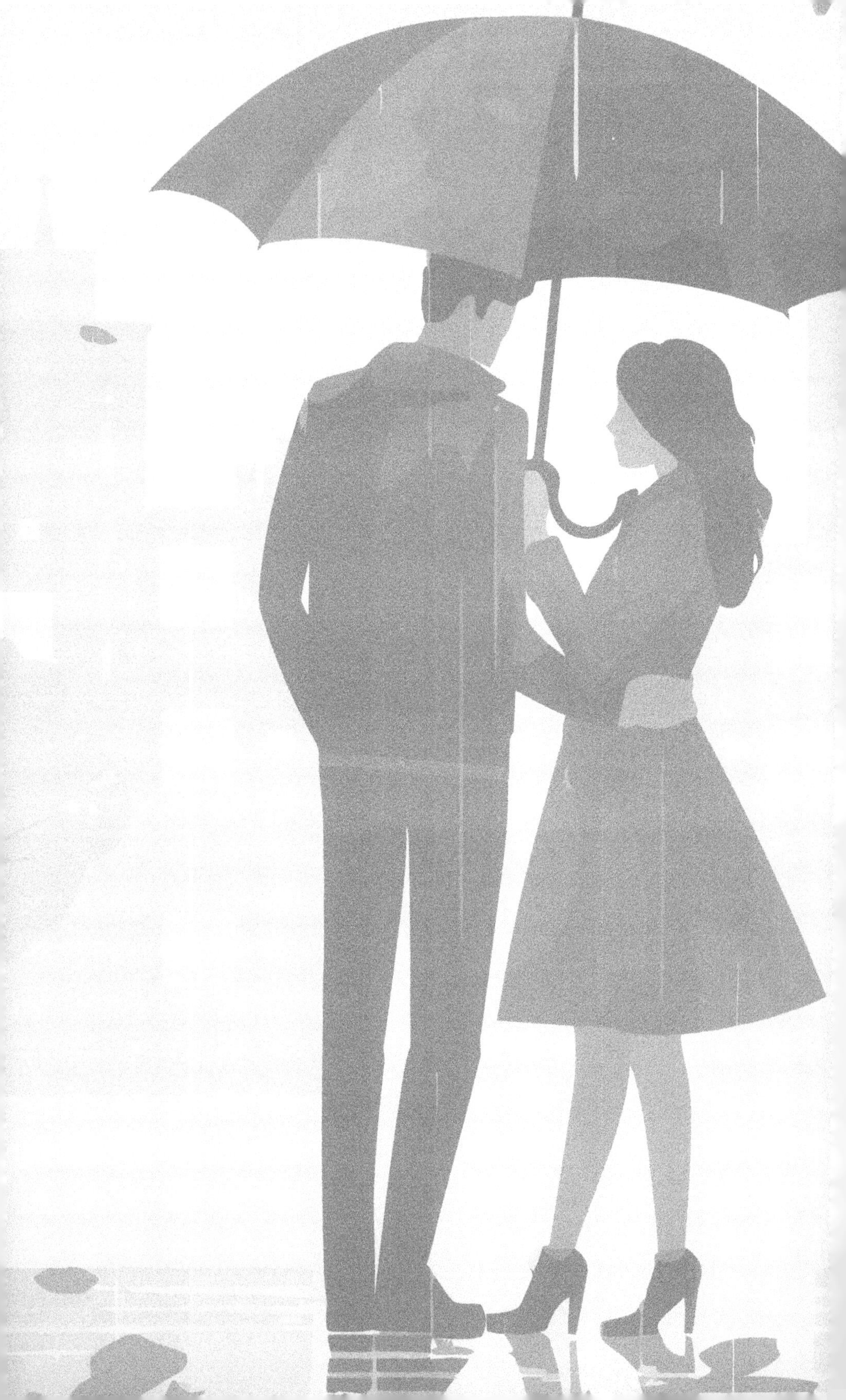

Chapter Twenty-Two

JAMES

The plan was for me to pick Tori up at her apartment.

I parked in a visitor's spot and waited for her in the lobby.

It seemed like I was a visitor everywhere with her.

The concierge watched me warily, as I paced from one end of the lobby to the other and back again, but didn't say anything. It was the suit and tie, I decided. A man wearing a suit and tie could get away with being just about anywhere.

I was a few minutes early, but it looked like she was going to be a few minutes late.

Maybe I should text her. Just to be sure I was at the right building.

Just as I was about to do so, one of the two elevators opened and Tori stepped off.

"Hi," I said, sliding my phone back into my pocket.

"Hi."

"You look beautiful."

She was wearing a slimming green sweater dress with a wide belt and little black moto boots. She had on makeup that accented her big green eyes framed by thick lashes.

She had brush dried her hair, leaving little loose curls on the ends. That took some time to do. I knew. I had sisters.

Her smile was relaxed.

She waved at the concierge who waved back as we headed outside.

It was a beautiful night with perfect weather for what I had planned.

"My car's right over here," I said, leading her over to the visitor's parking.

"Where's your truck?" she asked as we neared the sleek little black Maserati.

"I didn't bring it."

"You have two vehicles?" she asked as I opened the passenger door for her.

I laughed. "We've come a long way from our college days, haven't we?"

We didn't say much as we left her apartment building and drove across the bridge into town where we had reservations.

This was different from just lunch. This was an actual date.

I'd honestly never thought we would get back to this point. I'd known I wanted to, on a deep level, but the logistics were too complicated for me to consciously comprehend.

When I pulled up to the restaurant, three valets were there to open our doors and take my keys.

"Welcome back, Mr. Ashton," one of them said as I handed over my keys.

Going around, I took Tori's hand and tucked it inside the crook of my arm.

"I feel like I'm underdressed," she said.

"No," I said. "You're perfect."

The restaurant was noisy and crowded as it was every night.

The hostess, a young lady by the name of Cindy, looked up as we walked passed her. I nodded and she picked up the phone.

"We get to ride the elevator," I said, pressing the button.

"Okay." The doors opened and we stepped inside. "There's a restaurant up here?"

"There is. It has a stunning view. I think you'll like it."

I pushed the button for the fifteenth floor as the doors closed.

"Fifteen?" Tori asked.

"Trust me?"

"Yes," she said, but her brow was furrowed. Looking at it from her perspective, I could see where it would look rather strange.

We rode up to the fifteenth floor and stepped off.

A tall lean man in a tuxedo was there to greet us.

"Welcome Mr. Ashton," he said. "Dr. Graham."

Tori looked over at me with obvious questions.

I smiled. This was one of those good surprises.

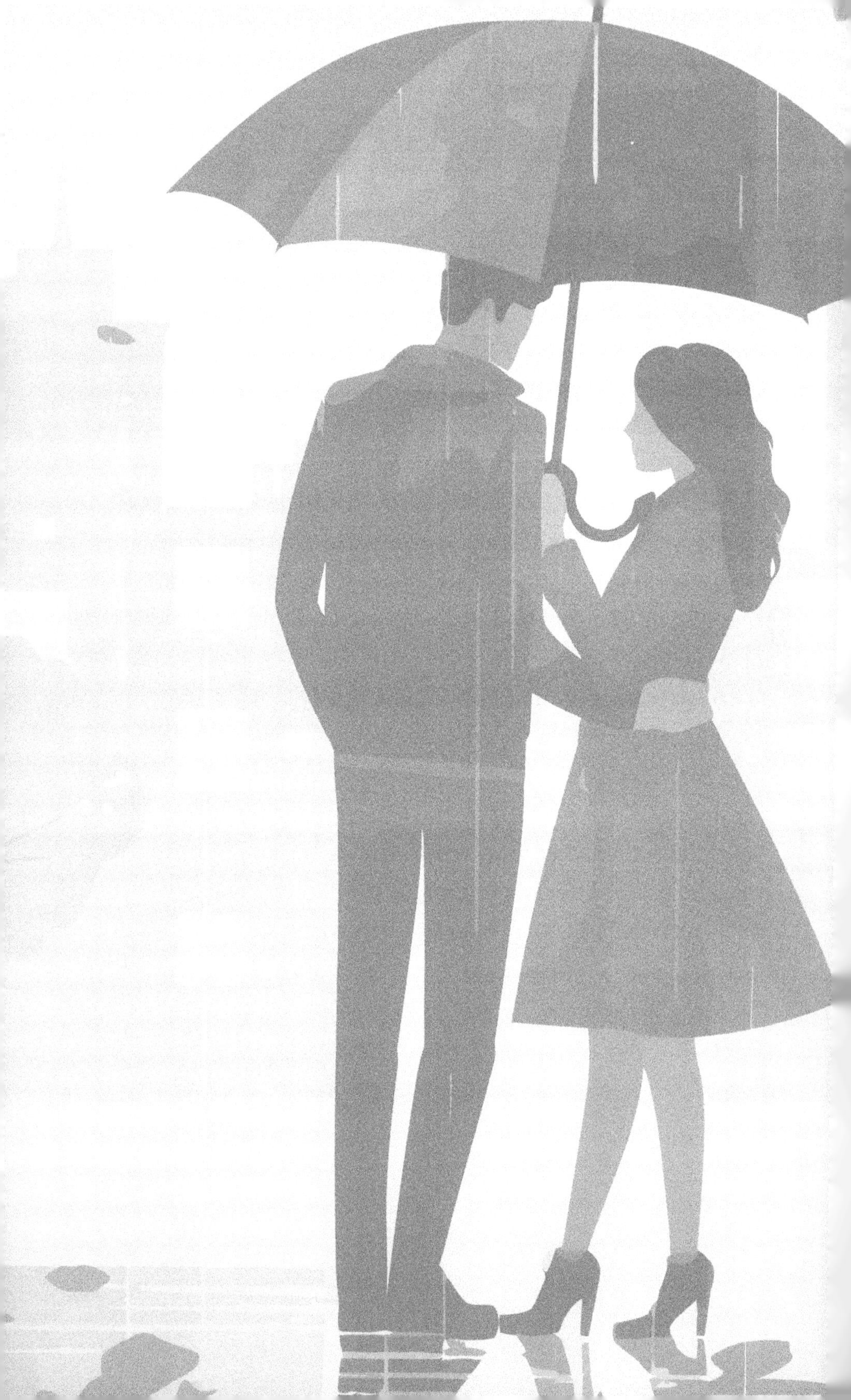

Chapter Twenty-Three

VICTORIA

We stepped off the elevator on the fifteenth floor.

The fifteenth floor that was actually the roof of the building.

Twinkling stars and a bright full moon as a ceiling. The light breeze tousled my hair and cooled my skin. From here we could see the city lights and lights from the bridges and the cars that crossed them.

There was one table with a white table cloth and candles and a vase full of freshly cut flowers. No other tables. No other guests.

A tall lean man wearing a black tuxedo greeted us with a white cloth draped over one arm and a bottle of wine in the other.

He greeted James by name, but he also greeted me by name.

James pulled out one of the chairs and held it for me while I sat.

Then he sat in the chair across from me.

The server turned over two glasses and filled them with water, then he held up the wine for James to see the label.

"Yes," James said. "That's good."

The server opened the wine and poured a touch in my glass.

"Try it," James said.

It tasted like vanilla and blackberries and cinnamon.

"It's good," I said. "Really good."

"Very good." The server poured wine into our glasses, set the bottle on the table, and left us.

I leaned forward.

"James? How does he know my name?"

James swirled the wine in his glass, looking quite pleased with himself.

"I made reservations."

I glanced around. There were trees and flowering plants. "This..."

"You don't like it?"

"No." I retuned my gaze to his. "I like it a lot. It's beautiful. I'm just... surprised."

"A good surprise, I hope."

"A very good surprise." I smiled. "But how?"

A helicopter passed overhead, its blades loud. City ambiance that we would barely notice on the ground.

"I know the owner," he said.

"You know...? Your father?"

"This is one of his buildings. His restaurants."

"I'm overwhelmed. It's beautiful."

"Since we didn't have a first date last time, I thought maybe we could have a memorable first date this time."

"Lunches don't count?"

"I guess we can call it our third date if you want to."

"Semantics," I whispered. "Whatever we call it, it's definitely memorable."

I placed my hand in his across the table and he laced his fingers with mine. I gazed into his clear ocean blue eyes and wondered how we ended up here.

"It's so good to see you again," he said.

"It's good to see you, too."

"Now," he said, looking up. "Our appetizers are here."

The server, I learned his name is Marvin, brought blackened shrimp and flaked crabmeat.

It was wonderful and it was decadent.

But most of all, it was the most romantic dinner I'd ever had and even more, it was with the one man I had never stopped loving.

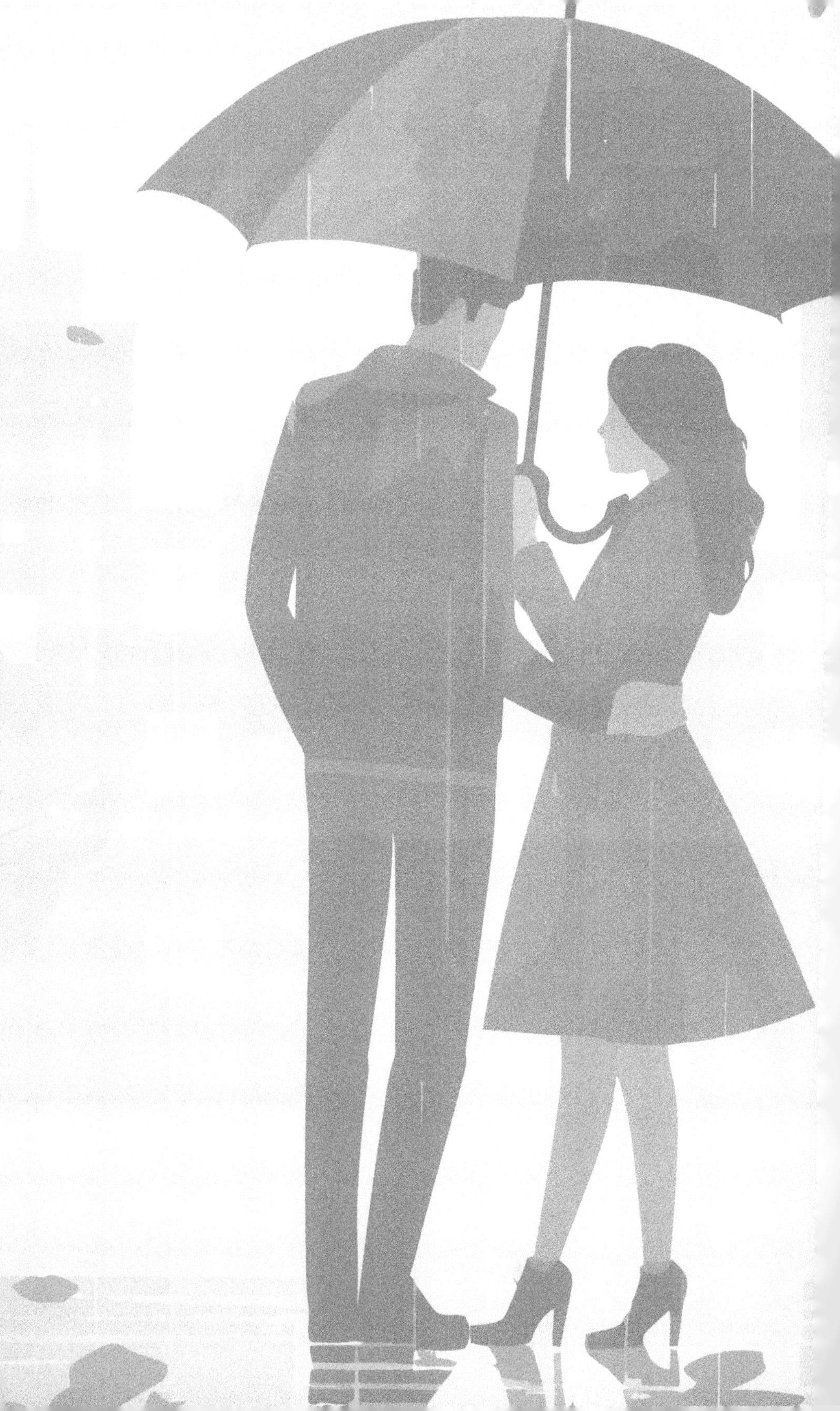

Chapter Twenty-Four

JAMES

The night was perfect for a rooftop dinner. The moon was full, the stars bright, and the city sprawled out below us in all its glory.

My phone vibrated in my coat pocket. It was the third time in the last thirty minutes.

I should have turned it off. I was here with Tori, enjoying a perfect dinner.

It was the perfect date.

"I need to turn my phone off," I said, pulling my phone out of my pocket and powering it down.

"Someone's calling you?" Tori asked.

"Yes, but it can wait."

"It might be important."

"It might be," I said. "But it can wait."

She took a little sip of her wine.

"I'd feel better if you at least checked."

"Seriously?"

"If something is wrong, you'll blame me."

"I would never blame you," I said, but now it was nagging at me. Something could be wrong. My grandfather had a heart attack last year and the memory was still fresh.

If nothing else, that was the one thing that swayed me to look.

I had two calls from my sister and one text message, also from my sister.

> BELLA
>
> Call me on your way home.

"It's just my sister," I said. "I can call her back later."

"If you need to call her, I understand."

"I don't need to right now. I just need to enjoy a lovely dinner beneath the moon and stars with an even lovelier young lady."

It was odd for Bella to call me when she knew I was on a date with Tori, but there could be any number of reasons why she wanted to talk to me.

Maybe she just wanted to know how it went.

It was still early and Bella usually stayed up late.

I put it out of my head, though, and focused on Tori.

"I can't believe you never got married," I said.

"I had a couple of proposals," she said. "Wait. I had three counting the student who proposed to me during class."

"You have to be making that up."

She shook her head. "I'm not kidding."

"How did that work?"

"I used to do this thing on the first day of class where they all wrote down one question about the class or about me, anonymously, and I would go through them and answer them. In front of the class."

"That sounds a bit risky."

She shrugged. "I reserved the right to not answer. Anyway, one of the questions was 'will you marry me?' It made the other students laugh."

"What did you say?"

"I don't know. I don't think I said anything. I think I just went on to the next question."

"Good," I said. "For a minute there, I thought you might be engaged."

Tori laughed.

Perfect. It was a perfect night.

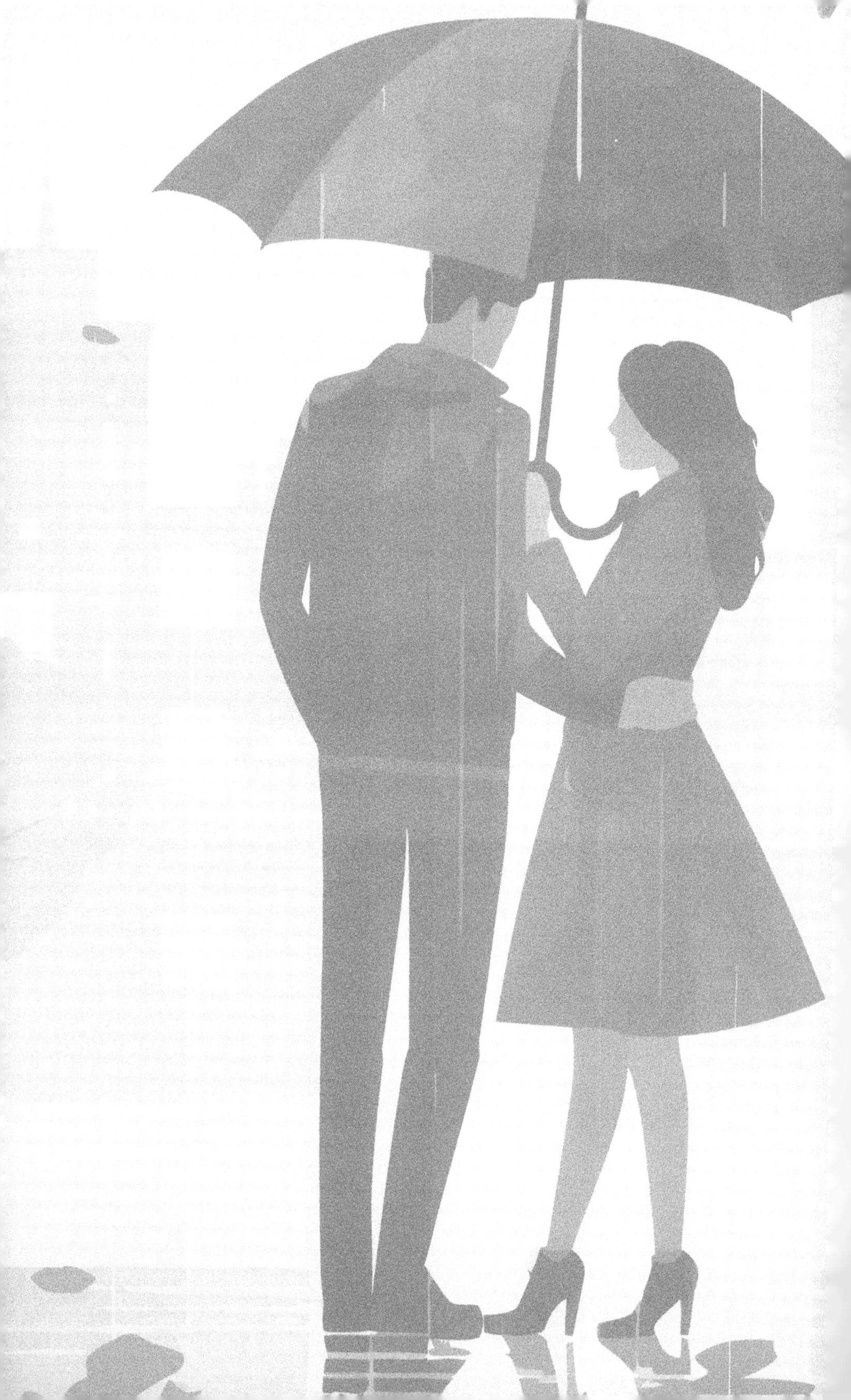

Chapter Twenty-Five

VICTORIA

After dinner, James drove me home, parking in the visitor's parking, and walked me inside.

He followed me to the elevator.

My neighbor, Wesley, with the big lab, joined us.

"How's Max?" I asked him.

"Mad at me for being gone all day," my neighbor said. "Does he bark when I'm not home?"

"I never hear him."

The elevator doors opened and we all stepped inside, riding up to the tenth floor together. James stood next to me. He smelled good. Like leather with the tangy scent of pine. Maybe cedar. And just a hint of jet fuel.

It was so easy to fall back into step with him again. Nothing in particular had happened to split us up. Nothing other than maybe distance.

We'd gone from seeing each other every day to phone calls and text messages.

Then I'd gotten busy. He'd gotten busy. Either I was working with patients or he was in the air.

It seemed like our communication got crossed and the more crossed it got, the less there was of it.

Time marched on and we talked less and less.

He flew out to Salt Lake once. He'd made a good effort. But I'd ended up being on call that weekend and one of my patients had a crisis.

I'd hardly seen him. I hadn't even been there when he had flown off.

Looking back, that had been the beginning of the end. Actually, I hadn't seen him again, so maybe it was actually the end.

I think he gave up on me and I didn't have the bandwidth to do anything about it.

My feelings were still there. They had simply gone dormant. Like flower bulbs in the winter that sprouted with the first hint of spring.

My feelings were like the bulbs. Just waiting for the warmth of the sun and James was the sun.

The elevator opened and Wesley stepped off with Max.

"See you later," he said. Max gave my hand a lick.

"Okay," I said, scratching the dog behind his ears.

Wesley and Max headed across the hall to their apartment, leaving me alone with James.

"I'm over here," I said, walking over to my door. I keyed in the code and the door clicked open.

Putting one hand on the knob, I turned around, my heart rate skittering up a beat.

James was standing there, right there. Looking at me with his bright blue eyes. Eyes that seemed to see right into my soul. Into the deepest, darkest corners of my being.

He saw into the part of me that had never stopped loving him.

Placing his fingers lightly on my chin, he ran a thumb across my bottom lip.

My eyes automatically fluttered closed and my neuronal pathways all rushed through pathways that had been dormant for years.

He leaned forward. I knew because I felt his breath brush my skin.

He kissed my forehead, then he eased back.

"I'll see you Saturday," he said.

"Saturday." I opened my eyes, still in a haze. "Right."

He took a step back.

He was leaving.

Right.

I turned the knob and stepped into my apartment.

I slowly closed the door and leaned against it.

I stayed that way until I heard the elevator open and close, taking him back downstairs.

James Ashton had never been known for moving slowly.

There was only one explanation. Either he never had been interested in picking back up where we left off or he had considered it, but changed his mind. Either way, I was getting the impression that I needed to guard my heart carefully.

But then there was Saturday.

I'd see him Saturday.

It was enough. For now.

And the fact that I was worried about it, told me that I was in trouble.

I had fallen right back under the spell of James Ashton.

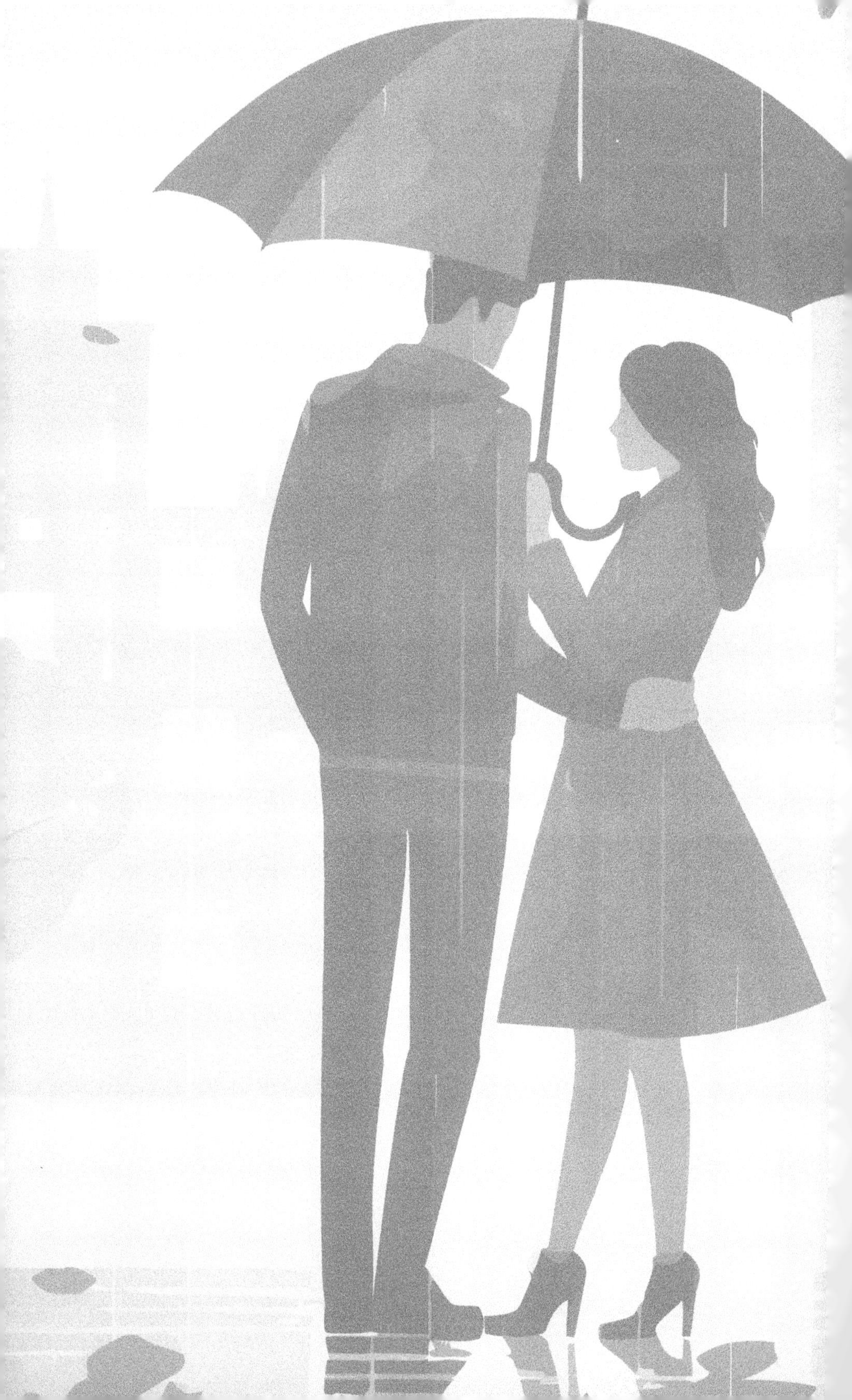

Chapter Twenty-Six

JAMES

I turned up the music and sang along as I drove home.

I could have kissed Tori. It would have been so so easy to just pick right back up where we had left off.

It would have been easy, but I wanted to take my time. I wanted to do it right.

Tori wasn't just a girl to carelessly date. She was Tori.

And that meant something.

Tori was the girl I wanted to marry.

I could see it all so clearly now. It had somehow escaped me all those years ago. I'd known it, but I had let that thought slip out of my hands.

This time I wasn't going to let it slip out of my hands.

This time I had to do everything right.

I pulled into the driveway and parked.

Tomorrow I would send roses to Tori's office. I had to do everything by the book.

Unfortunately, or maybe fortunately, I was out of practice with doing things by the book. For all I knew, things had changed.

I would ask Bella. She would know. Bella had her pulse on today's culture. More than anyone else I knew.

As I stepped out of the car, I remembered that I was supposed to call Bella on the way home.

Well. I was here now.

I bounded up the stairs and reached for the front door.

It opened, Bella standing on the other side.

"Sorry," I said. "I forgot."

"It's okay," she said, stepping out of my way. She looked troubled. Not in crisis mode, but troubled.

I took off my coat and hung it in the coat closet.

Then turned around.

"What's so urgent?" I asked.

"You had a visitor while you were out."

"A visitor? Who?"

I wasn't expecting anyone.

I followed her back to the kitchen.

She waited until she reached the kitchen island. Then turned, leaning against it.

"Tiffany."

"Tiff—" What the? "Why would she come here?"

"Sit down," she said.

I slid out a barstool and dropped onto it, all the while trying to think of what if anything Tiffany could want with me. And why would she come here? She had no reason to come here.

"What did she want? We don't have any unfinished business."

"Actually," she said. "You kind of might."

Again. I could think of nothing that we had left unsettled. Our accounts. She had her car and the apartment.

By all accounts, we had been mutually content with the outcome of the annulment. She had actually come out better than she had been going in, financially anyway.

"James," she said. "Tiffany's pregnant."

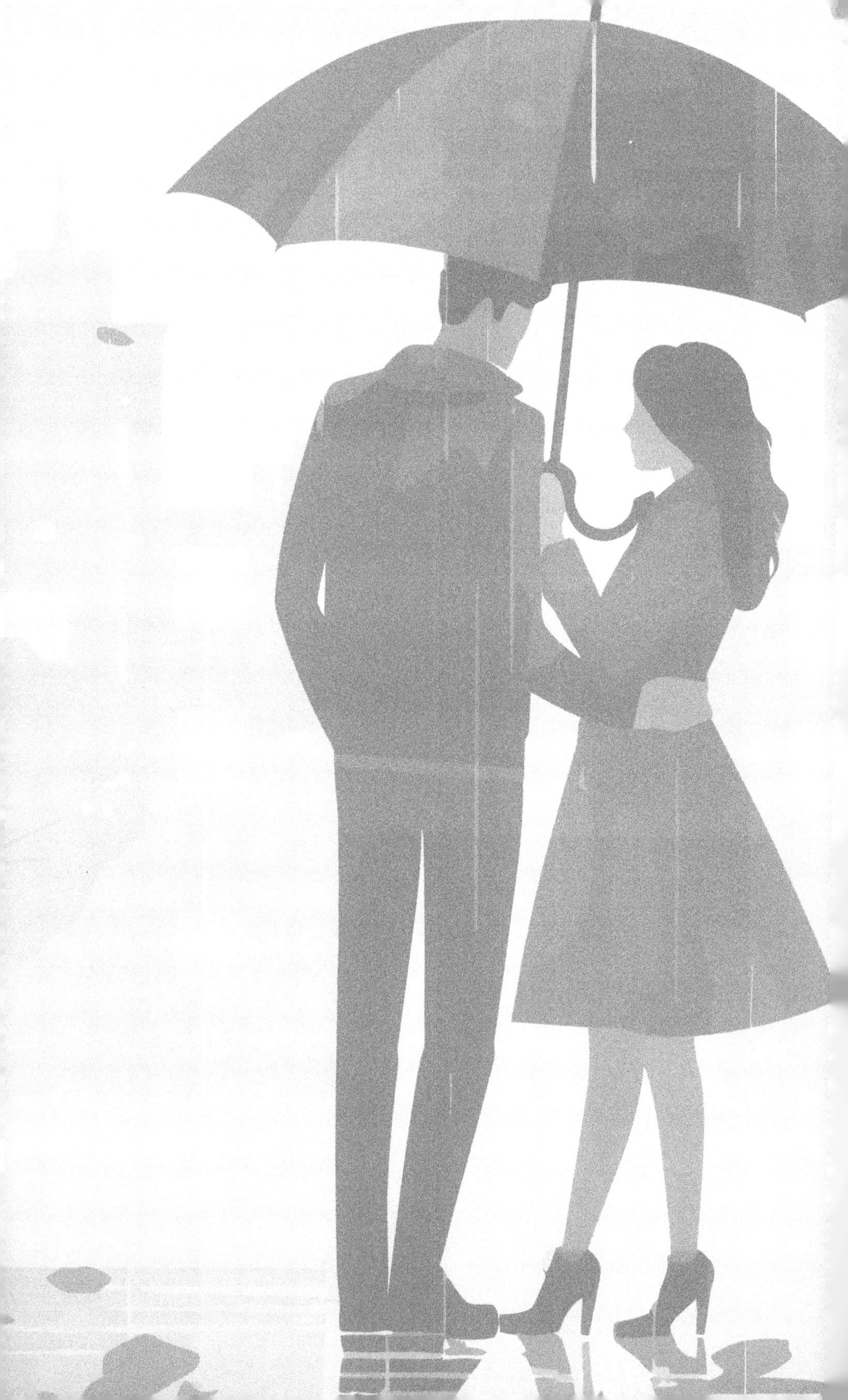

Chapter Twenty-Seven

VICTORIA

The next day I was busy.

First of all, I had two classes. One of them was a test, so I had some time to think as I watched the students struggle over their answers.

I, of course, thought about James.

Before last night I had never had a rooftop dinner, nor had I ever had a restaurant to myself. It wasn't technically the whole restaurant. It was just the rooftop dining room.

I had looked it up. There were usually a dozen tables available on the rooftop at any given time, all by reservation.

James had used his connections—his grandfather or his father—for us to have the rooftop to ourselves.

If his intent had been to sweep me off my feet, it was working.

Two of my best students turned in their tests quickly.

"Enjoy your weekend," I said.

But then James had confused me. He had walked me to my door like the gentleman that he was. I'd thought he was going to kiss me.

It was almost like he changed his mind at the last minute and decided not to. Instead, he had kissed me on the forehead.

A simple chaste kiss. So sweet it made my heart ache.

A chaste kiss wasn't what I wanted from him. I knew what it was like to kiss him. I'd taught him to kiss the way I liked it. Sweet and deep.

But fifteen years was a long time. He had no doubt kissed a lot of other women. He had even been married.

Other women would have influenced the way he kissed.

I couldn't fault him for it. I had kissed other men, too. Not that anyone kissed me the way James did.

"Dr. Graham?" One of my students asked, coming up to stand next to the desk where I sat.

I felt my cheeks flush. I'd been caught thinking about kissing.

"Do you have a question?" I asked.

"Did you mean this?" he asked, pointing to question seventeen. "Or this?"

I read the question.

"It's straightforward," I said. "Don't try to read anything into it."

He still looked confused.

"Go with your first instinct," I said. "Remember the example I gave in class."

"Right," the student said, realization dawning on his face. "Thanks."

My thoughts wound right back to James.

We were going flying Saturday. Maybe he would kiss me then.

I was like a schoolgirl. Daydreaming about the cute guy.

I watched for James as I walked across campus back to my office.

As I sat at my makeshift metal desk, answering emails, I watched the door for him.

I halfway expected him to randomly show up. Maybe take me to lunch.

But lunch came and went.

Since I had halfway, unofficially, waited for him to show up, I skipped lunch.

Feeling rather ridiculous for thinking he would just show up, I found some crackers in my desk and ate them before my afternoon graduate class.

When I got to class early, John was already there, sitting up front, Sigmund at his feet.

"How are you Dr. Graham?" he asked.

"I'm good," I said as I unpacked my computer and powered it up. "How are you John?"

"Still trying to get used to being in a strange classroom."

"You'll get used to it," I said. "It's what I've been telling myself anyway."

John smiled. "I'm sure we'll adapt."

I was proud of John. Despite him having his own comfort dog—or maybe because he had his own comfort dog and thus understood what it was like to need comfort—he was going to be a good counselor.

"Are you okay?" he asked. "There's something different about you."

"I'm okay," I said. "Thank you for asking."

There was definitely something different going on in my life.

I'd reconnected with my college sweetheart. Had lunch with him twice and a dinner date—definitely a date—with him.

I'd thought he was going to kiss me, but he had seemed to change his mind at the last minute and kissed me on the forehead instead.

John had come a long way.

And he was going to go far.

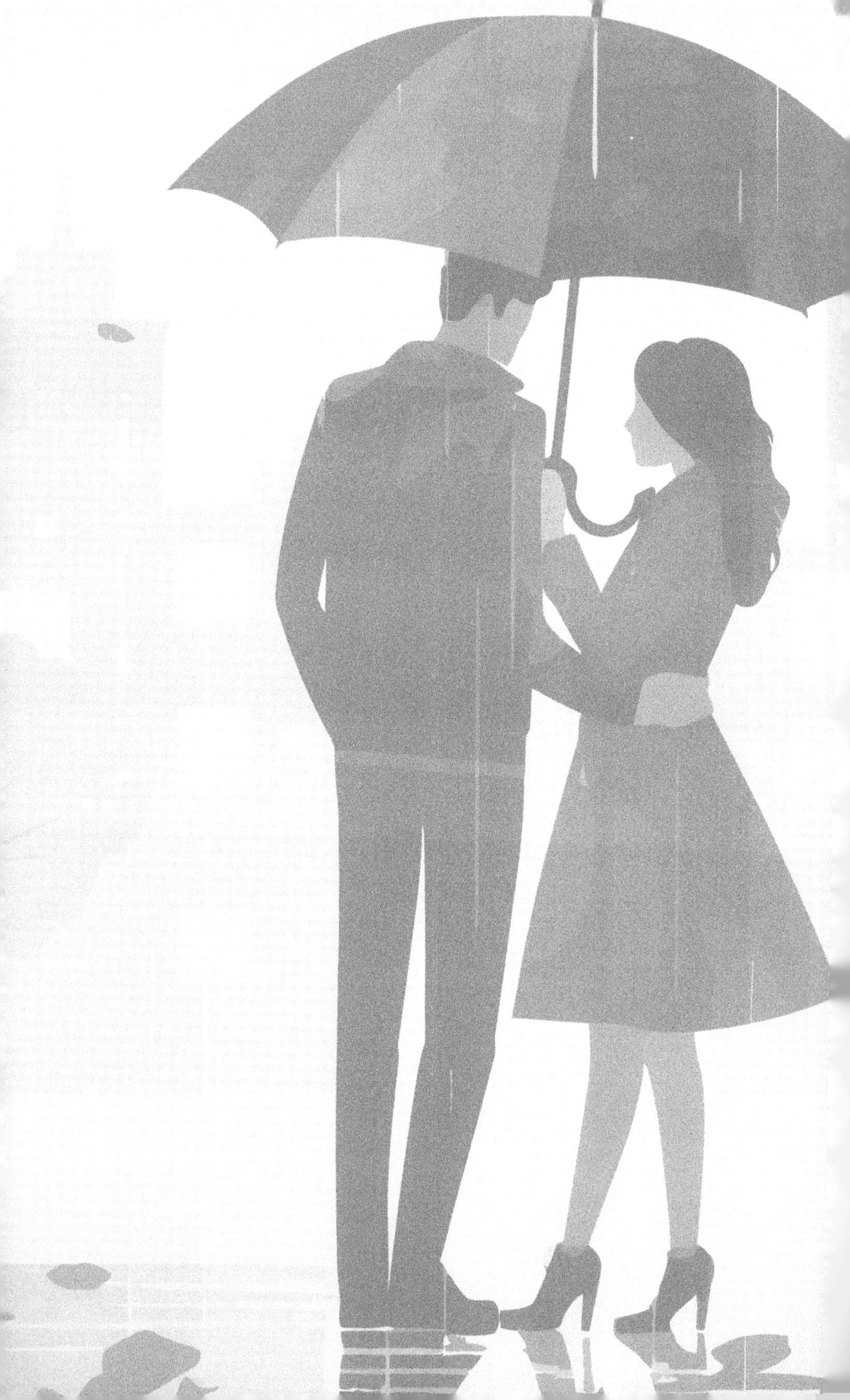

Chapter Twenty-Eight

JAMES

I had an early morning flight, so I was up before sunrise and on my way to the airport.

Since I had gotten in late last night, I'd had very little time to digest the news that Tiffany had shown up at our house claiming to be pregnant, much less getting in touch with her.

As I made the flight to Philadelphia, I contemplated what I was supposed to do with this information. Since she had shown up on my family's doorstep looking for me, I had to worry about what she wanted.

Maybe she just wanted to tell me.

But I wouldn't be so lucky.

She wanted something else.

I didn't know if she was seeing anyone else yet. If she wasn't, then she was probably looking to me to step into the role of father.

I would, of course. It was the right thing to do.

It didn't matter that I had considered myself fortunate to have gotten out of my relationship with her so easily. But if she was pregnant, then that changed all that.

I wouldn't be nearly so disconcerted about it if I hadn't just reconnected with Tori.

The timing was all off.

In fact, it couldn't be worse.

If I had found out about Tiffany being pregnant before stepping back into Tori's life, I might not have pursued Tori so quickly. I might have let her go after rescuing her from the building. I might have, at least, gone about it differently.

Tori didn't deserve that in her life.

She deserved to have someone free and clear. Someone who could put all their attention on her.

It had been bad enough that I had been married, but this was worse.

This was so much worse.

I needed to talk to Tiffany, but also I needed to figure out what I was going to do.

I would do the right thing. Doing the right thing did not have to mean being with Tiffany again, but it did mean that I would need to be a father to the child.

I did some math in my head. Depending on how far along she was in her pregnancy, it was possible I was the father. Remotely possible, but possible, nonetheless.

June.

Yes. It was possible.

But why was she coming to me now?

Why not months ago?

I did the external preflight check, then boarded the plane to wait for my passenger.

He was a man I had known a long time. A friend of my grandfather's. Dr. Mike Anders.

Mike was a very successful older man. A psychiatrist who only saw patients by special request now.

He always rode in the copilot's seat and he was a talker. That was probably a good thing. I needed some distraction from my own thoughts.

The limo showed up just as I was finishing up my preflight checklist. I checked the radar one more time. Verified the flight plan.

"Good morning, James," he said, coming into the cockpit and taking his seat. "I appreciate you getting up this early for me."

"Always a pleasure," I said. "You know I don't mind."

While I closed and secured the door, he harnessed himself in.

"How are you doing?" he asked.

"Good," I said automatically, even though it wasn't entirely true.

Mike sat quietly while I taxied out to the runway and took off.

He kept his eyes on his phone while we achieved ground effect. Then as we reached altitude, he turned his attention to me.

"What's bothering you, Son?" he asked. Mike was a very perceptive man.

"Just... I don't want to burden you with my problems."

"If I can't help an old friend, what good am I?"

I looked over dubiously at him.

"You know how much I hate drama."

"Come now," Mike said. "We've got about two hours. Tell me what's on your mind so I don't have to sit over here and make things up."

I laughed. "Okay, but don't say I didn't warn you."

"Whatever it is," he said. "I can promise you, I've heard worse."

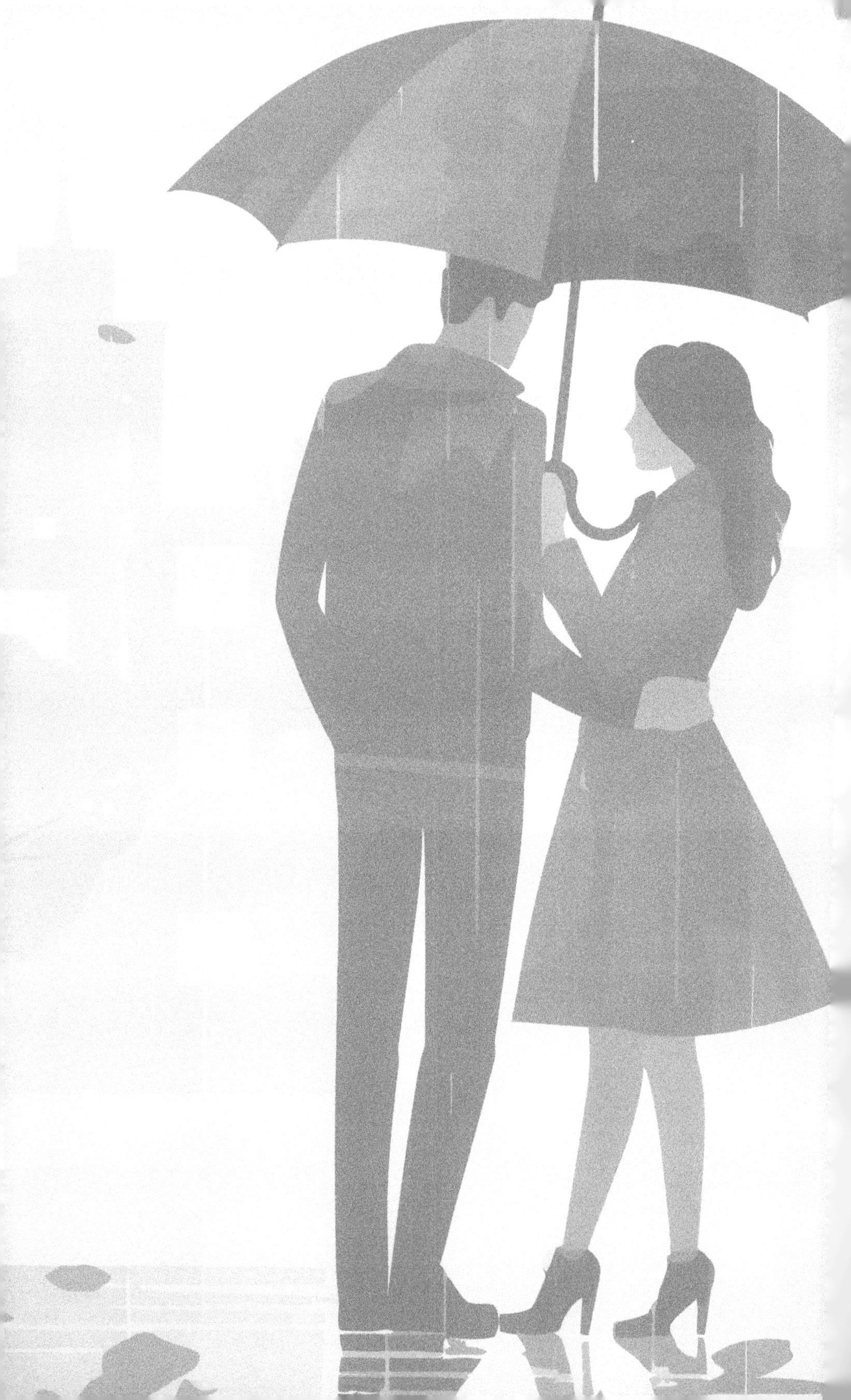

Chapter Twenty-Nine

VICTORIA

On the way home from the university, I stopped by the market and picked up a frozen pizza. While I was there, I picked up a bouquet of bright yellow and pink flowers.

Juggling everything, I pushed the elevator button with my elbow.

I needed to have a nice quiet evening. Spent like a normal person. Eating my frozen pizza and reading my novel.

Last night had been one of those anomalies. It had been like a fairy tale. Private seven course dinner on the rooftop beneath the stars.

Tonight I would be back down to earth. Back to normal.

Recalibrate myself.

I'd gotten so carried away I had missed lunch, thinking James would show up. He would have—back when we were dating. Back then we had lunch together every day. And dinner. We'd done everything together.

I couldn't expect that now.

Years had passed. Things were different.

Plugging my phone in to charge, using that as an excuse to check for messages, I sighed. No messages. I hadn't heard from James all day.

Day after tomorrow we were supposed to go flying.

If he didn't forget.

I took the pizza out of the wrapper, and set it in the oven, right on the rack, to cook.

With dinner in the oven, I took out a glass vase and took my time arranging my flowers in it.

I hardly ever bought myself flowers, but I'd found that buying them for myself took away any expectation or disappointment from not getting flowers from a man.

I'd just set them on my coffee table and was admiring them when my doorbell rang.

I glanced at the clock on my wall. Who would be coming here this time of night?

A little part of me hoped it was James. No one had called from downstairs, but maybe they remembered him from last night and let him up anyway.

With my pulse quickened, I opened the door.

"Momma. What are you doing here?"

"Can't a mother check on her only daughter?" She swept inside. "Especially when that daughter doesn't return her calls."

"I'm sorry," I said. "You called while I was in class and I..." Forgot. I forgot. "I was going to call you after I ate. I missed lunch."

"You forgot," she said sweeping through my kitchen on her way to the living room.

"I would have remembered," I said. And I would have. I was a good daughter. I just wasn't in the right frame of mind right now.

"Frozen pizza?" she asked, catching sight of the box I'd left on the counter. "Really?"

My mother was something of a snob. Even now she was wearing a powder blue pencil skirt and matching jacket that would make Grace Kelly proud. Attorney Graham.

I was something of an anomaly in my family of attorneys. Even though I was a PhD, my family sometimes without actually saying it, made me feel like they were disappointed in me.

When the three of them—my mother, father, and my brother—got together and talked shop, I was most definitely on the periphery.

My brother's wife was a stay at home mom and it didn't seem to bother her not to be part of their conversations.

"Who gave you flowers?" she asked.

"I bought them for myself," I said, straightening.

"Victoria," she said. "You shouldn't have to buy yourself flowers. Didn't you have a date last night?"

"I did. But that has nothing to do with buying flowers for myself."

"Hmm," she said, sitting on my sofa. "Come. Sit. Let me look at you."

"I'm fine," I said, sitting across from her.

Instead of looking at me, though, she seemed fixated on the flowers.

"Was your date with another college professor?" she asked.

"No." I knew what my mother thought about my dating other professors. She didn't consider professors to be professional men. They were, of course, but not up to my mother's standards.

She narrowed her eyes at me. Considered.

"You're dating one of the firemen who rescued you."

She was too close for comfort.

Was I that boring in her eyes? That I couldn't find someone who wasn't a professor or a fireman who rescued me?

I straightened my back. I was not going to give her the satisfaction of letting her know how close to right she was. That I was dating the fireman who rescued me. Even if he was only a volunteer fireman.

"I'm dating a pilot."

She didn't say anything for a moment.

"You're dating that Ashton boy again." It wasn't even a question. Just a statement.

I caught my breath.

My mother had never liked James. A pilot was somehow down the food chain, even below professors.

"I went on a date with James."

My mother shook her head.

"Why? After all these years? I thought you had moved on."

"Momma. He's a good person."

"A good person would not break your heart."

"I was the one who moved away," I said.

"It was for the best," Momma said.

I was getting a headache. Anytime Momma tried to talk to me about anything, I got a headache.

The timer went off.

"My pizza is ready," I said. "Do you want some?"

Mother glanced at her phone. "I have to go. I'm meeting your father."

It had always struck me as odd that my parents set up meetings with each other. Not dates. I could have understood dates.

It was more like they were business associates than a married couple.

"Okay," I said with a shrug and got up to turn off the oven.

I put mitts on my hands and pulled it out of the oven. Momma didn't know what she was missing. It looked wonderful to me.

"Victoria," she said with obvious resignation and judgement in her voice. "Find yourself a good man. A man who can support you properly and settle down. Buying yourself flowers and having frozen pizza for dinner is no way to live."

My mouth open, I watched her walk out my door.

Slowly removing my oven mitts, I closed my mouth.

"And please explain to me, Mother, why exactly you came here tonight. Other than to criticize everything about my life."

I took a slice of pizza, slid it onto a paper plate—just to rebel against my mother even though she wasn't here to see it, settled onto my sofa, and ate while I read my book.

My life was perfectly fine.

And it was even better with the possibility of James being in it.

My mother had no idea what she was talking about.

And besides, I didn't ask for her opinion.

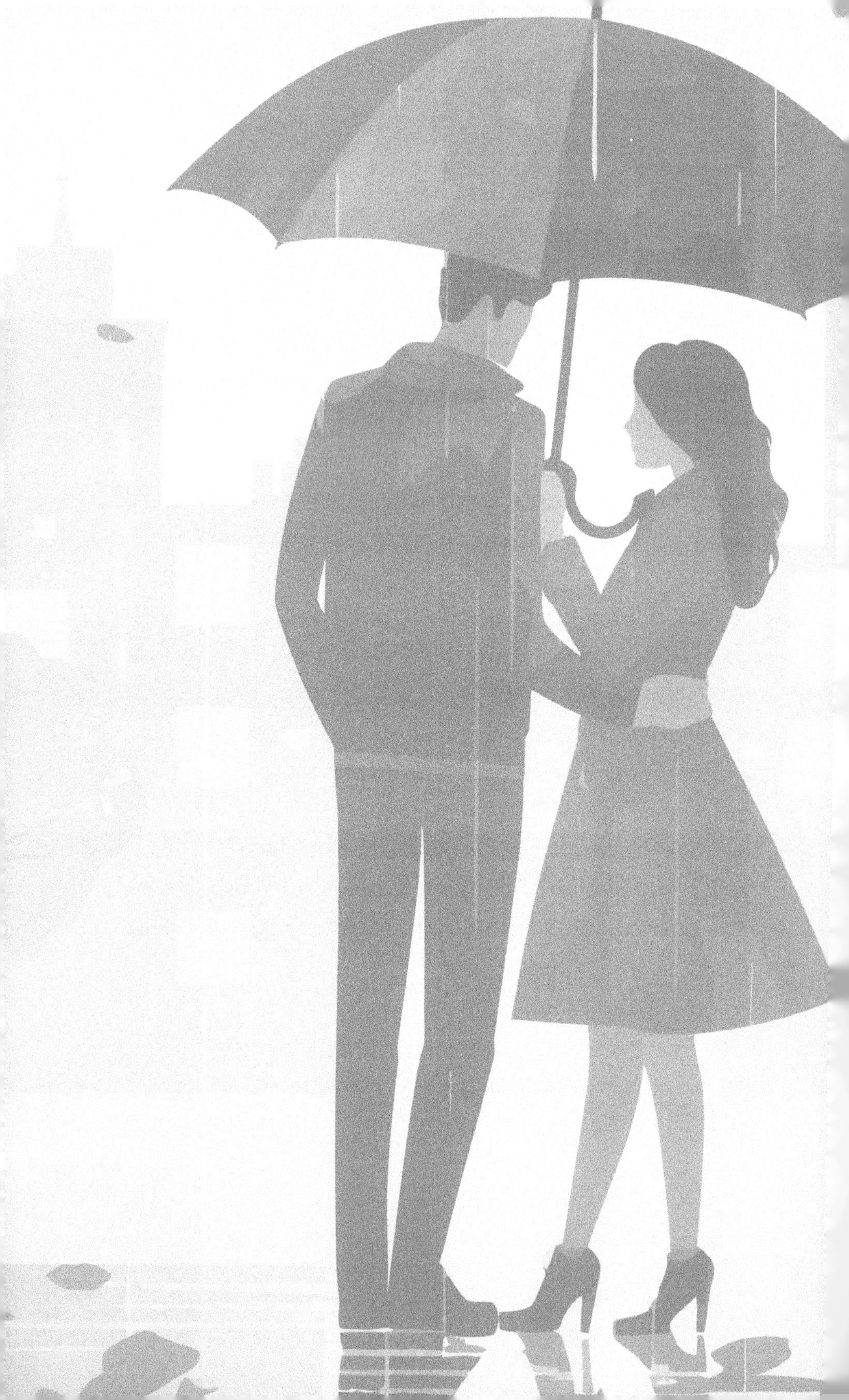

Chapter Thirty

JAMES

I ended up unexpectedly spending the night in Philadelphia.

Mike needed a return flight in the morning and it didn't make sense for me to fly back to Pittsburgh only to have to turn around and pick him up only hours later.

Fortunately, I kept an overnight bag with me.

I hadn't really meant to, but I had told him about Tiffany and about Tori.

He hadn't given me any advice. He didn't do that.

But he was a good listener.

As I walked along the streets of Old City, Philadelphia, I called Tiffany.

She kept her cards close and I knew nothing more than I'd known before I called her.

We agreed to meet tomorrow I got home.

As I talked to her, I realized I didn't really trust her. That gut feeling was a big part of why we had gotten our marriage annulled after only one month.

I found a Pub and ordered a beer.

I liked Philadelphia. The historicalness of it.

It was a good place to go for a romantic getaway.

As I sat there, watching people come and go, I knew that it was Tori I wanted to bring here.

She would like it. She might be a true psychologist, but she appreciated history. There was a lot of history here. More than Pittsburgh.

I wondered if she had ever been here.

I toyed with the idea of texting her. Asking her.

But it somehow didn't seem right. I needed to get this thing with Tiffany straightened out before I put my focus back on Tori.

I was too distracted.

Maybe on the flight home tomorrow, I'd come right out and ask Mike what he thought I should do.

I trusted his judgement and in this particular situation, I trusted it more than I trusted my own.

I'd thought I was finished with Tiffany. I thought that chapter of my life was closed.

I had happily reopened the chapter on Tori and was more than ready to turn that page.

But just as that was looking promising, Tiffany had come back into my life.

I could not in good conscience ignore Tiffany.

Not if the baby was mine.

There would be a DNA test for sure.

I'd forgotten to send Tori flowers today.

Tiffany had disrupted my whole thing and it had been going so well with Tori.

The romantic dinner on the rooftop.

I should have kissed Tori. She would have let me. I had no doubt about that.

But I didn't want her to kiss me because it was what we had done before. I wanted her to kiss me because she wanted a future with me.

I was going for a future. Not wanting to relive the past.

And I was putting far too much thought into this.

Tori was Tori.

There was no separating the past and future with her.

I had a plan.

I would see Tiffany tomorrow. Sort things out. Explain to her that I would do what I had to do, but I had moved on.

She should have moved on by now, too.

Of course, a baby would preclude that, wouldn't it?

I finished up my beer and walked back to my hotel.

I would figure it out.

My family would be behind me. Bella already knew, so it wasn't a secret.

My mother wanted grandchildren, but this wasn't exactly the way she wanted them.

It wasn't the way I wanted to give them to her either.

It would sort itself out.

Tori was still my end game. That hadn't changed. Wouldn't change.

It would just take a lot more work. It wasn't fair to Tori. But it was what I had to offer.

The thing I could hope for the most was that Tiffany had moved on.

Surely that wasn't too much to hope for.

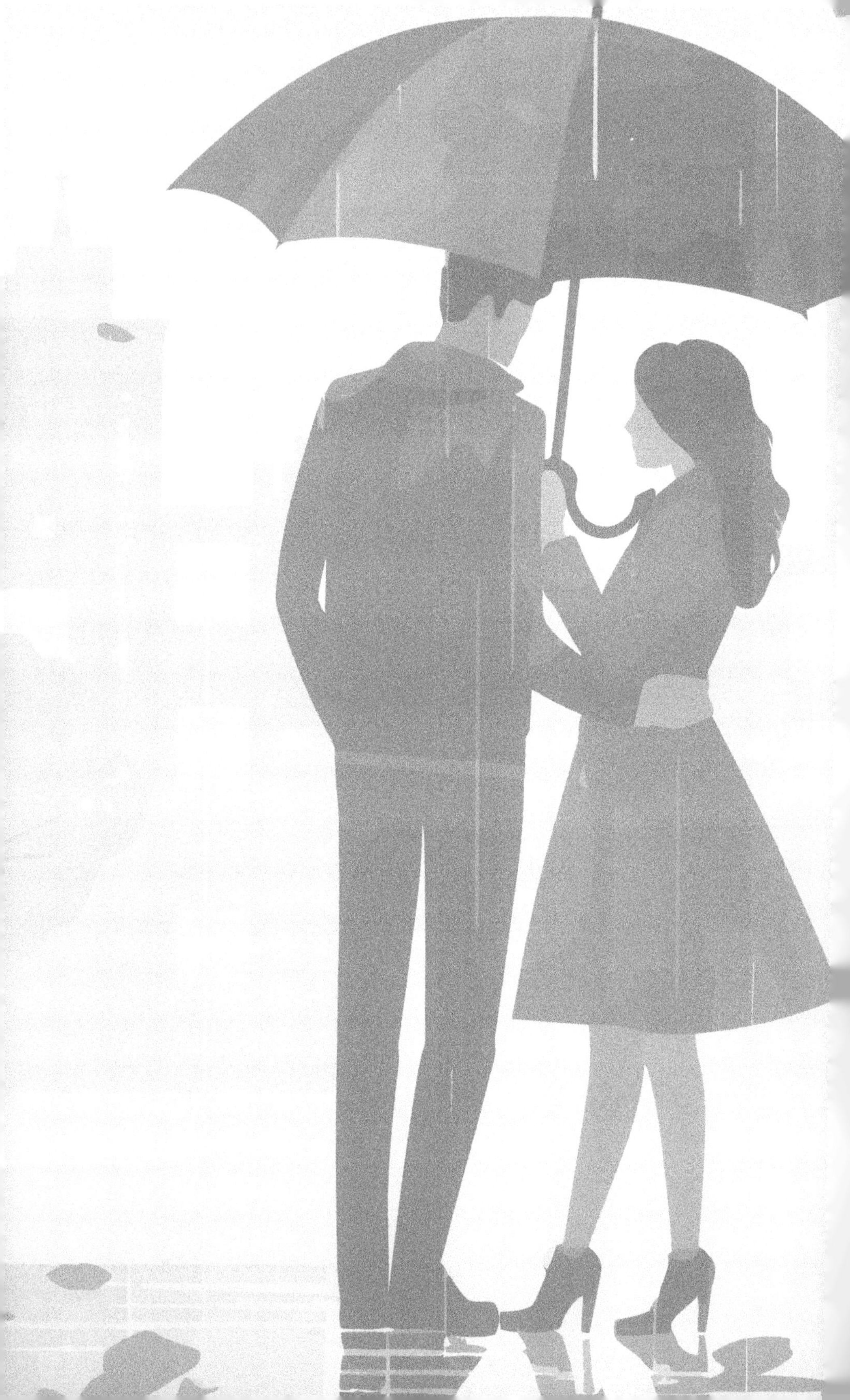

Chapter Thirty-One

Victoria
Saturday Morning

I'D FLOWN with James before. Back when he was a student. He was a licensed pilot before we even graduated with our undergraduate degrees.

But that was a long time ago. A very long time ago.

Since then I had flown commercial the few times I had flown.

And even then when I had flown with James, we'd flown in a little prop plane. A two-seater Cessna, to be exact.

But the airplane waiting on the tarmac was a very sleek, very impressive Phenom with the Skye Travels logo splashed across the fuselage in bright red.

James had given me the whole experience. He'd sent a limo to pick me up from my apartment. To drive me out to the airport.

We drove right out onto the tarmac and stopped next to the airplane.

James, his arms crossed, stood there next to the stairs leading up into the airplane.

He was wearing his pilot's uniform. A black suit with a black tie. White shirt. Pilot's cap and dark sun glasses.

The pilot's uniform was a far cry from his fireman's uniform.

He wore the look well. Wore them both well.

After the driver came around and opened my door, I stepped out and walked toward James and the airplane.

The scent of jet fuel was strong and the breeze was cool. A commercial jet left the ground and flew overhead, its engines deafening.

James slid his dark glasses off and met me halfway across the distance.

He picked me up at the waist, my feet leaving the ground, and twirled me around.

I grabbed hold of his arms and caught my breath as he set me back on my feet.

"Hi," he said.

"Hi."

"How was your ride?"

"It was good. I could have driven."

"And I could have picked you up," he said, but you would have missed out on half the experience."

I didn't care so much about the experience. I cared about seeing James again.

But I appreciated the effort and the sentiment behind it.

"It's a big airplane," I said. "Bigger than I expected."

"It's a Phenom," he said.

"I know," I said with a little smile.

He raised an eyebrow.

"You might recall that I wasn't the only one teaching someone what I was learning."

"No," he said. "I gave you a lot of information. I just didn't expect you to remember it."

Of course he wouldn't.

What he couldn't have known was that I paid attention to everything he told me. I remembered not only the different types of airplanes, but also different types of clouds and even the weather patterns he had taught me.

Truth be known, I could probably have landed a plane back then. Now. Probably not so much.

I went up the stairs first. They weren't quite as stable as I would have expected and I was glad I had on my flat canvas sneakers.

If not for the full flowy skirt, I would have felt underdressed. I had debated between jeans and a dress. Gone with a compromise. A long full skirt in shades of green and a little white sweater.

I thought my outfit was pretty cute and on top of that, it was comfortable.

"Come sit in the copilot's seat," he said, steering me toward the cockpit.

I sat down and fumbled with the four-point harness.

He sat down next to me.

"Want some help with that?"

"I can do it," I said with more confidence than I felt.

"Okay," he said with a little shrug and began going down the preflight checklist.

"Maybe a little help," I said after a few minutes.

James laughed and leaned over to easily clip me in.

"You make it look so easy," I said.

"Experience," he said. "You'll get better."

I smiled. Just three little words, but they soothed my heart, leaving me feeling hope that this was not just a one-time thing.

I didn't want it to be just a one-time thing.

I wanted him to be my forever guy.

As he took the plane up to altitude, I thought maybe, just maybe it was possible.

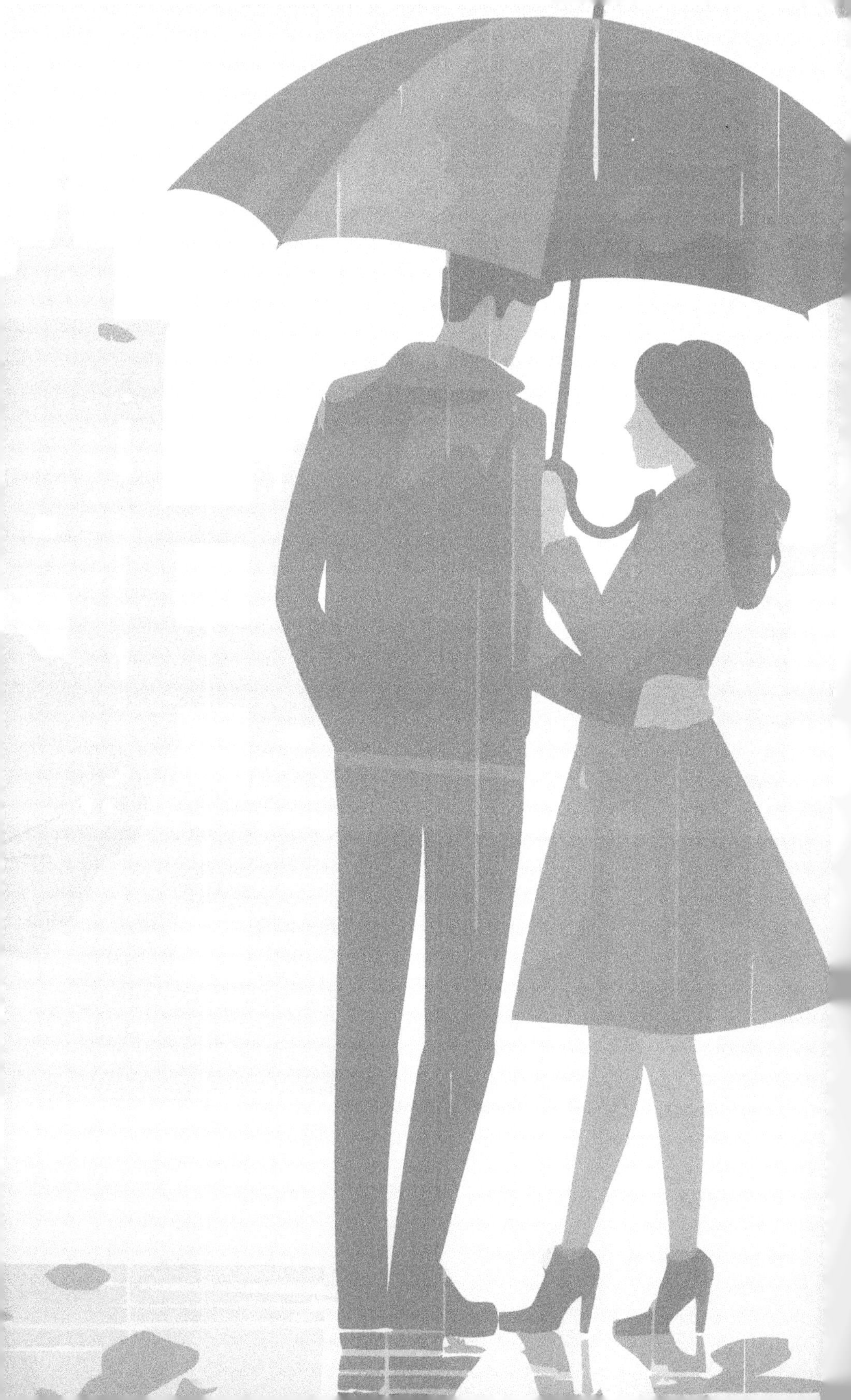

Chapter Thirty-Two

JAMES

I took her to Mackinac Island.

One, I wanted a quiet place to talk to her and two, I wanted to share one of my favorite places with her.

The Phenom was almost too big for the little runway on the island, but I had some experience in landing here.

I'd arranged to have a taxi waiting for us.

A taxi on Mackinac Island consisted of a horse and buggy driven by a man in a tuxedo.

It was a beautiful time to visit the island.

Maple leaves were in full glory red, lining the road from the airport toward town.

The air was crisp and clean with fall.

"Is this your first time here?" the driver asked.

"It's her first time," I said.

"Well, welcome to Mackinac Island."

"Thank you," Tori said. "It's lovely."

I'd given her the tour from the air, pointing out the Grand Hotel and the roads with no cars allowed. Pedestrians. Bicycles. Horse and buggies.

We went straight to the Grand Hotel. The historical Grand Hotel held boasting rights to the longest porch in the world.

"We're having lunch here," I said. "Then we can take a walk around the lake."

"You have everything planned out," she said.

"I didn't think you would mind."

"It's rather nice to have a day when I don't have to make the decisions."

"Good." I was hoping she would feel that way.

It could have gone either way.

As we stepped inside, the Hotel Orchestra took us back to days gone by along with the formally dressed servers.

We took a seat looking out toward the straits.

A ferry packed with tourists headed across the water toward us.

Tori leaned forward toward me.

"Is this where they filmed that movie with Christopher Reeve?"

"Somewhere in Time," I said. "Yes. You've seen it?"

"It's been a while, but yes."

She looked around, seeing it differently.

"I'm going to have to watch it again," she said. "This is just... I'm just speechless."

All through lunch I worried.

I worried that once I told her what I had to tell her, she wouldn't think things were quite so wonderful.

Nonetheless, I forced myself to focus on the here and now.

We were here, together, in one of my favorite places.

"We have to have some of their pecan balls."

"Pecan balls?"

"Trust me on this," I said.

The vanilla ice cream, pecans, and fudge rolled together into such a wonderfully simple gooey deliciousness was one of those things that had to be experienced.

And to my delight, Tori loved them as much as I did.

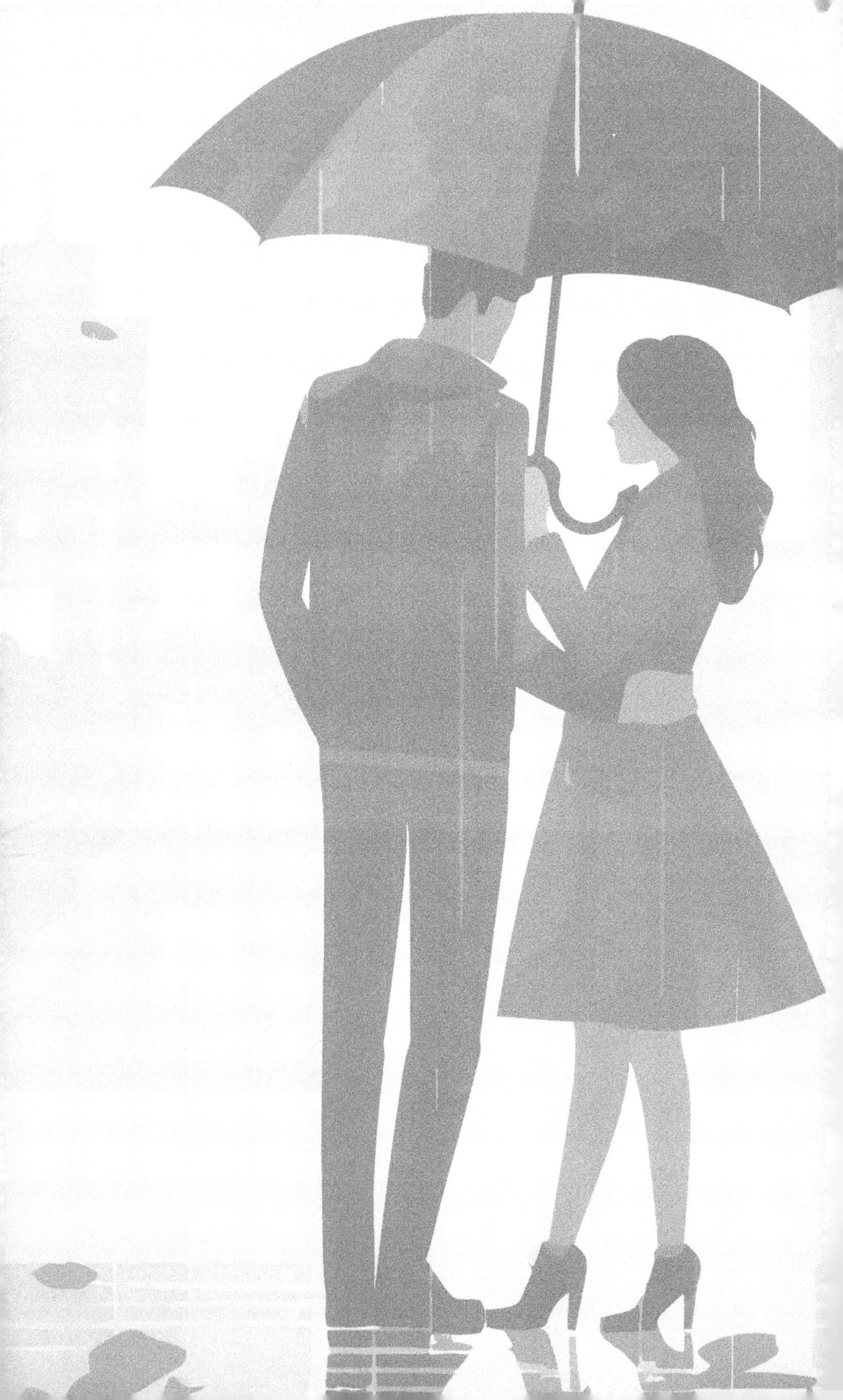

Chapter Thirty-Three

VICTORIA

I'd never been to a place like Mackinac Island.

From all accounts, this was the perfect time of year to visit. The sun was warm on my head and the breeze had a pleasant chill to it.

The maple trees were ablaze with color as they prepared to shed their leaves for winter.

The island was crowded with weekend tourists, which, I suppose, we were part of.

Since there were no cars allowed on Mackinac, James and I walked from the Grand Hotel to the little town of Mackinac.

Once again, I was more than glad that I had worn comfortable shoes.

I expected James to point out things as we went, but he was uncharacteristically quiet.

We reached the edge of the water and found a bench to sit on.

Gentle waves drifted in, reminding me of relaxation exercises I used with patients.

"Thank you for sharing this with me," I said. "It's beautiful."

"It's one of my favorite places. But…" He put a hand over mine. Laced his fingers with mine. "I need to talk to you about something."

Something in the way he said it, had alarm bells going off in my head.

But instead, I smiled. "Sure. You can talk to me about anything."

"I hope you mean that," he said, squeezing my hand."

"You're worrying me just a little," I said.

"I don't mean to. I just need to tell you something. Something unexpected and unfortunately it might involve you."

"Okay."

"Remember I told you I was married and got an annulment?"

"Of course. Last fall, right?"

"That's right."

He waited while an older couple with a frisky black lab, an adult sized puppy, walked past us.

"She came to my house and talked to my sister. While you and I were on our date." He took a deep breath. "I met with her yesterday."

"What was it about?"

I tried to distance myself. To put on my counselor hat, but it wasn't working. My heart was pounding and I wasn't able to keep my emotions out of it. Not this time.

Instead, I imagined all sorts of things.

"She wants you back?" It was the worst case scenario as far as I could tell.

That had to be it.

And he was telling me because he was getting back with her. He'd promised me a plane ride, so this was it.

"It's not that," he said. "Even if she did, I'm interested in someone else."

"Right." I nodded and looked away.

He smiled. "You silly."

"Me?"

Our hands still linked, he kissed my palm.

"Before we go too far, I need you to know that she might be pregnant."

"But..." I tried to put the dates together.

"It's remotely possible," he said. "We're having a paternity test done."

"You can do that during pregnancy now." I remembered teaching about that in class. I'd just never considered how important it could be in real life.

"You said this affects me?"

"Yes. If the baby is mine, then I'll have to be involved. I don't know how much. But if the baby is mine, I have obligations."

"Of course."

"I'm telling you this because I want us to make this work this time around. I don't want to lose you again."

My breath hitched. I could hardly believe he was saying the things I wanted to hear. Or rather a modified version of them. His ex-wife being pregnant was not something I had imagined, much less expected.

"But before you decide about me," he said. "I wanted you to know what you might be getting into. I hope you'll at least wait until the test results come back to decide."

"I—"

He placed a finger lightly over my lips and looked into my eyes.

"Don't answer now, okay? Think about it. Wait for the test results."

I nodded. "Okay."

"I want you in my life. But it's only fair that you know."

I wanted to answer him now.

I knew what my answer was.

But he wanted me to wait.

So I would wait.

I understood why he wanted me to wait on the test and why he wanted me to think about it. If he was going to be a father with someone else, that was a big thing. A lifetime thing. Not just a divorce or an annulment. But a child changed everything.

A child was forever.

So for now I would keep my thoughts to myself.

And I would wait.

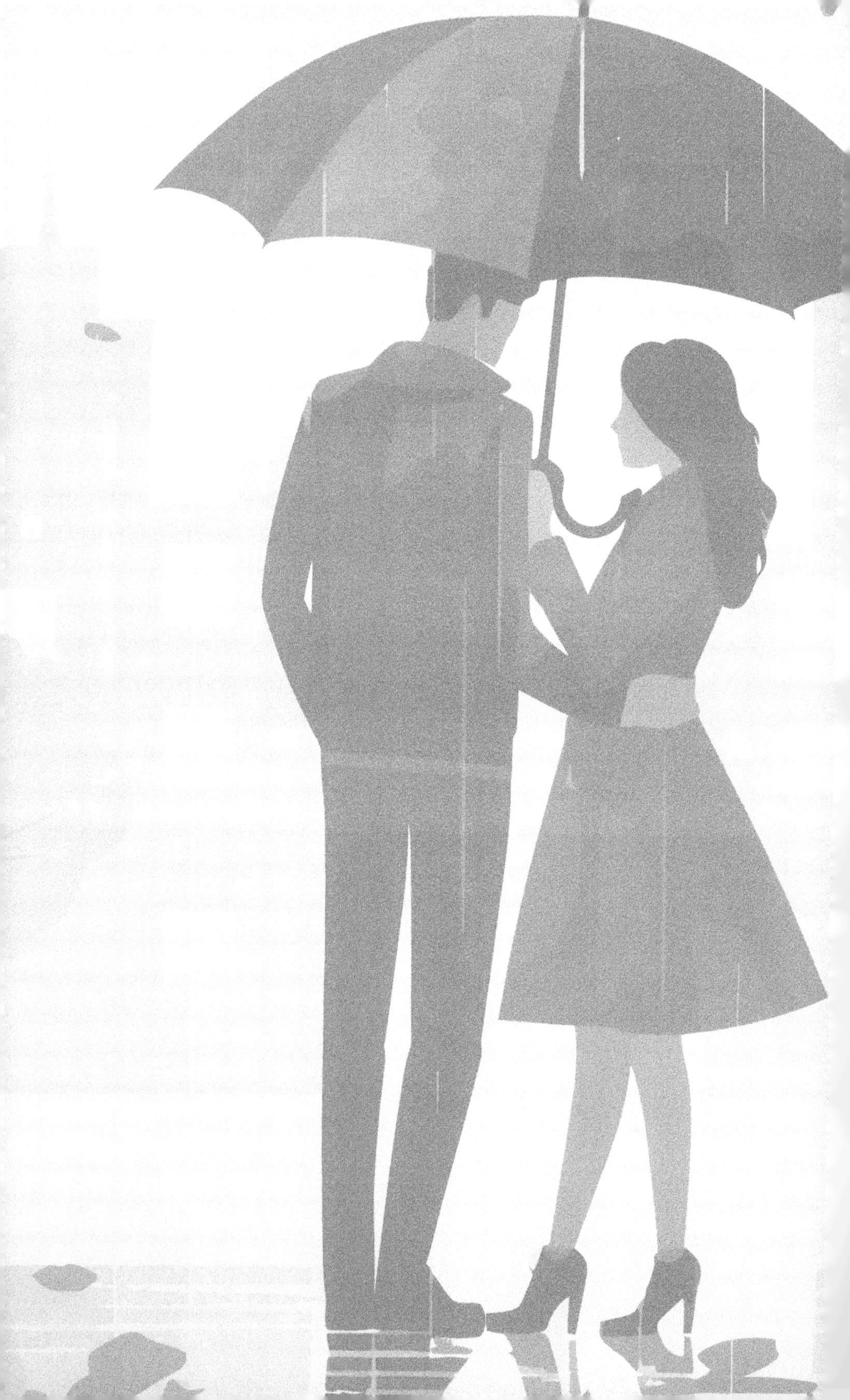

Chapter Thirty-Four

JAMES

Maybe Mackinac wasn't the best place for telling Tori about Tiffany's pregnancy after all.

For me, at least, it cast a shadow over the trip. Over my favorite place that I wanted to share with Tori.

But now it was done. It was out there.

We rode back to the airport beneath the maple trees with their bright red leaves in relative silence. Just the steady clip clop of the horse's hooves and the crush of the wheels on the pavement.

If I hadn't been so adamant that Tori not tell me her thoughts, we could have talked about it.

It had been Mike's idea to go ahead and tell Tori. Well. Maybe in all fairness, it hadn't been his idea so much as an option that he put out there.

It had made sense, so I went with it.

I hadn't expected it to kill me to not talk about it with Tori after I told her.

The not talking about it had been my idea, so I forced myself to stick with it.

We'd have the paternity test back in a few days. Then I would know more.

I didn't want secrets with Tori.

I'd never had secrets from her and I wasn't going to start now.

Starting a relationship off with secrets made no sense. It wasn't what I wanted to do.

Even if it destroyed our relationship, I'd had to tell her.

She had a right to know if she was going to be a stepmother.

As we neared the airport, I noticed a bruising of dark clouds against the sky. I'd been so preoccupied with telling Tori about Tiffany, that I hadn't noticed and for once I hadn't obsessively checked the radar.

I pulled out my phone and pulled up the weather app.

There was an unexpected storm rolling in.

"Is it as bad as it looks?" Tori asked, looking over my shoulder.

"I think so," I said, pulling up our flight plan.

"We have to err on the side of caution."

"We wait then," she said with a little nod.

"Look." I pointed to the future radar of Pittsburgh. "If we wait until the storm passes, there is no way we land in Pittsburgh tonight."

She looked into my eyes with those siren green eyes of hers.

"We're trapped," she said.

"Trapped is a rather dramatic word," I said. "But yes. We have to stay here tonight."

Without a word, she pulled out her phone and started looking for rooms on the island.

I liked that practicality about her. She'd always been calm in the face of stress.

The driver turned the carriage around and we headed back toward town.

"Have you found anything?" I asked.

She was frowning.

"The Grand Hotel has no rooms available. Apparently people are here to see the trees."

"They are pretty," I said, looking at the maple trees, their leaves ablaze with fiery red.

She clicked to another site.

"There's one opening. A bed and breakfast on the water."

"That sounds good."

She looked up at me with an unreadable expression.

"They only have one room."

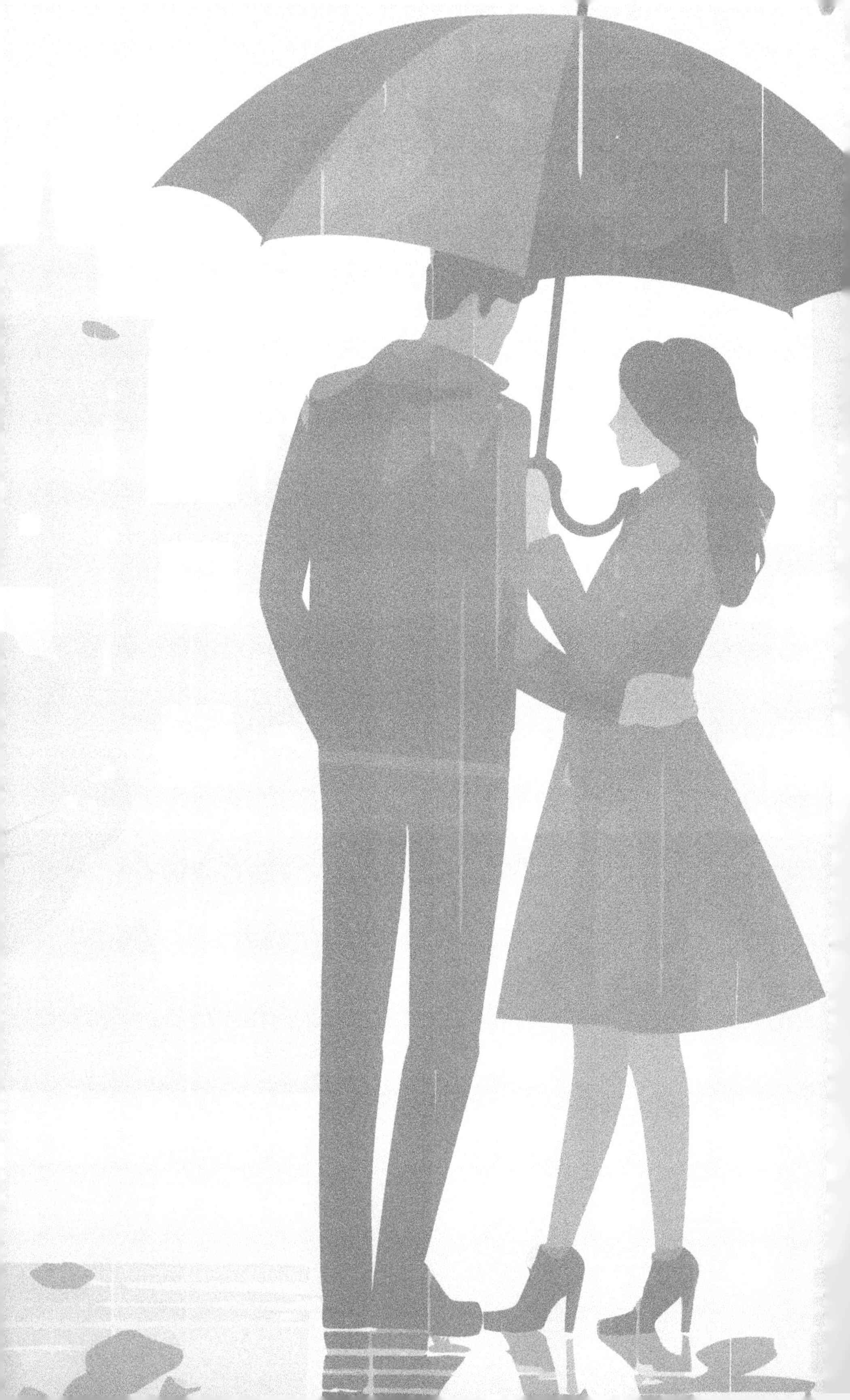

Chapter Thirty-Five

JAMES

The little bed and breakfast room was actually a little cottage, probably a maid's quarters at one time, behind a Tudor-style mansion on the other side of town, at the edge of the water.

It was about the size of a studio apartment. One room with a little kitchenette and a bathroom.

One bed and one sofa. All in the same room.

This wasn't part of the plan.

Not that it would have been a bad plan if I'd planned it.

A night spent on Mackinac Island was a very unexpected bonus.

There was one spot, a front window with a little dinette set in front of it that looked out over the lake.

From here we could watch the storm roll in. The black clouds making their way across the lake brought wind and lightning along with the sheets of rain.

We definitely did not need to be flying in this weather. As Noah Worthington—Uncle Noah—was known to say, there were old pilots and there were bold pilots, but there were no old bold pilots.

A very wise man, Uncle Noah.

Since our hostess had left a bottle of wine and two glasses on the table, we opened it and sat down at the little table to watch the storm.

I regretted telling Tori about Tiffany and the possible pregnancy. I needed to tell her, but I needed to tell her in Pittsburgh, in some ordinary place, not here. Not on this beautiful magical island.

"My mother came to see me," Tori said after a sip of wine.

I winced. Her mother had never liked me. I wasn't up to her standards. Both Tori's mother and father were attorneys who represented people who flew on private jets, not people who chauffeured them through the air.

"What did she want?" I asked.

"She doesn't think I should date you."

I must have given her a look.

"She figured it out," Tori said. "I didn't tell her."

"Well, that's not surprising." A flash of lightning lit up the room, quickly followed by a rumble of thunder.

"She also doesn't think I should buy flowers for myself and eat frozen pizza."

I laughed. "Good to know it isn't just me she doesn't approve of."

"Sometimes I don't think she approves of anything in my life. Or even me at all."

"She just wants what's best for you."

"I never thought I'd hear you defending her."

"Not defending," I said. "Just understanding."

"Huh." She took another sip of her wine.

"Well," I said. "My family loves you, so you're welcome at our house anytime."

A sadness crossed over her features. It was fleeting and if I hadn't been watching her, I would have missed it.

I put a hand over hers.

"Tori," I said. "Are you okay?"

"Of course," she said. "It just—I'm okay." She gave me a smile that was meant to convince me that nothing was bothering her, but I saw right through it. Something was most definitely bothering her.

It could be what I'd told her about Tiffany or it could be something else entirely.

Whatever it was, I wanted to make it go away.

I didn't know how to do that though.

Not now. We weren't kids anymore.

Life wasn't nearly as simple as it had been back when we were too young to appreciate it. Youth is most definitely wasted on the young.

The storm should pass through in time for us to walk downtown for dinner.

Maybe I could still turn this thing around.

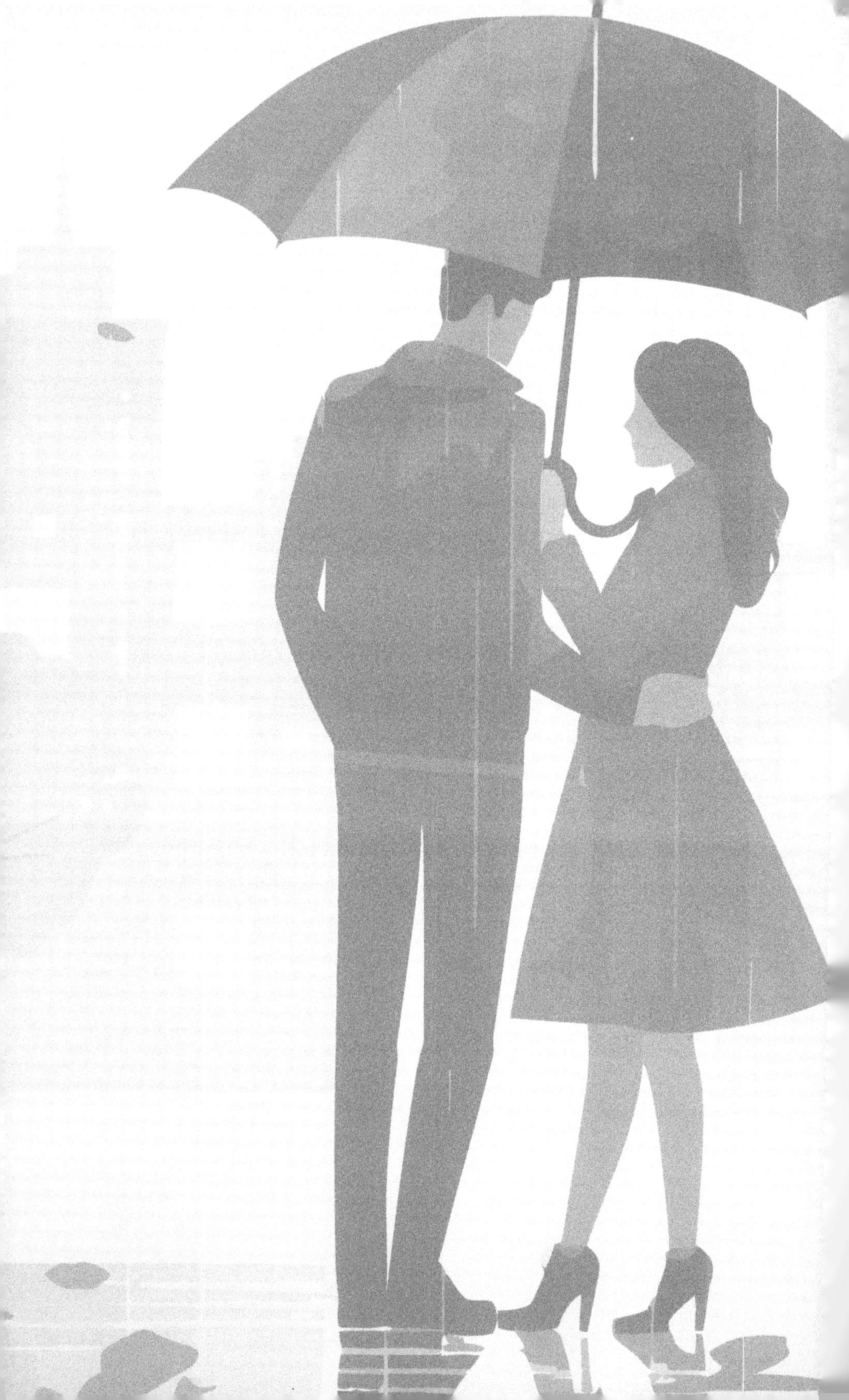

Chapter Thirty-Six

VICTORIA

I was talking too much. Telling James about my mother and how she didn't want me to date him.

My mother had no say over who I dated. I was an adult, for God's sake.

And now I'd gone and told James.

It was because I was feeling nervous about being here with him.

He and I had spent the night together a lot of times. But it had all been kissing and cuddling. Nothing more.

I was a little envious of Tiffany. She'd experienced an intimacy with James that I hadn't.

I'd always thought that would come later.

I had not expected life to come between us first. Or at all.

Now fate had brought us back together.

When I thought about him having a child with someone else, it twisted me up on the inside. How was I supposed to deal with that?

How was I supposed to decide if I wanted to be in a relationship with James when he might have a child with someone else?

Did I even really have a choice? He seemed to think it was a choice. If he thought I had a choice, he didn't know me as well as he thought he did.

As the lightning flashed outside, I considered reality. I was thirty-five years old.

The odds of me finding a thirty-something guy who didn't have an ex or a child was next to zero. And if I did, I'd probably wonder what was wrong with him.

People in their thirties were supposed to have experienced life. Relationships. It was normal.

He'd been up front with me and I appreciated that.

He said he didn't want to lose me again. He wanted me in his life.

Those words were burned into my brain like a bright light of hope.

What I didn't know, though, was what he meant.

Was he telling me because he felt like he had to? Or did he really really want me back in his life?

Maybe he wanted me back in his life as a friend.

Maybe he thought of us as friends.

I only thought that because he'd had the chance to kiss me and he hadn't.

My thoughts weren't making a whole lot of sense right now.

There was a magic on Mackinac Island. As a psychologist, I considered myself practical and not fanciful, but I knew what I felt.

Maybe it was the island. Maybe it was just spending time with James again.

Whatever it was, it had me confused and looking for answers. Not finding them in the swirl of wine in my glass, I looked up.

With the storm raging around us, I gazed into James's eyes.

"James," I whispered, my heart in my throat.

He swept a hand along my cheek.

"Why are you crying?" he asked.

I swiped at my eyes. "I didn't know I was."

But I should have. I should have known I was crying. I felt the emotion welling in my throat and it was only natural that it would spill out of my eyes.

"Come here," he said, pulling me into his lap.

I rested my head on his shoulder, my hands fisted in his shirt. And I cried.

He gently rubbed my back, my hair, soothing.

I cried for what could have been. What was. What could be.

I cried for the lost years and the life we could have had.

I cried for what the future could hold because I wanted it so badly I could taste it.

Finally, my tears spent, I caught my breath.

"I'm sorry," I said. "I don't know what happened."

"It's okay," he said, sweeping damp hair off my face. "You can cry on my shoulder anytime."

"Thank you." I smiled a watery smile. I felt raw and exposed. Vulnerable.

"Tori," he said.

I sighed as he pressed his forehead against mine. I didn't think I could bear it if he didn't kiss me like he had not kissed me before at my apartment door.

I raised my chin until our breath mingled.

I caught a glimpse of his face as lightning flashed around us. His expression was intent, but other than that, I couldn't read it.

When our lips touched, I didn't know if I kissed him or if he kissed me.

In the end, I knew I would never know and I also knew that it didn't matter.

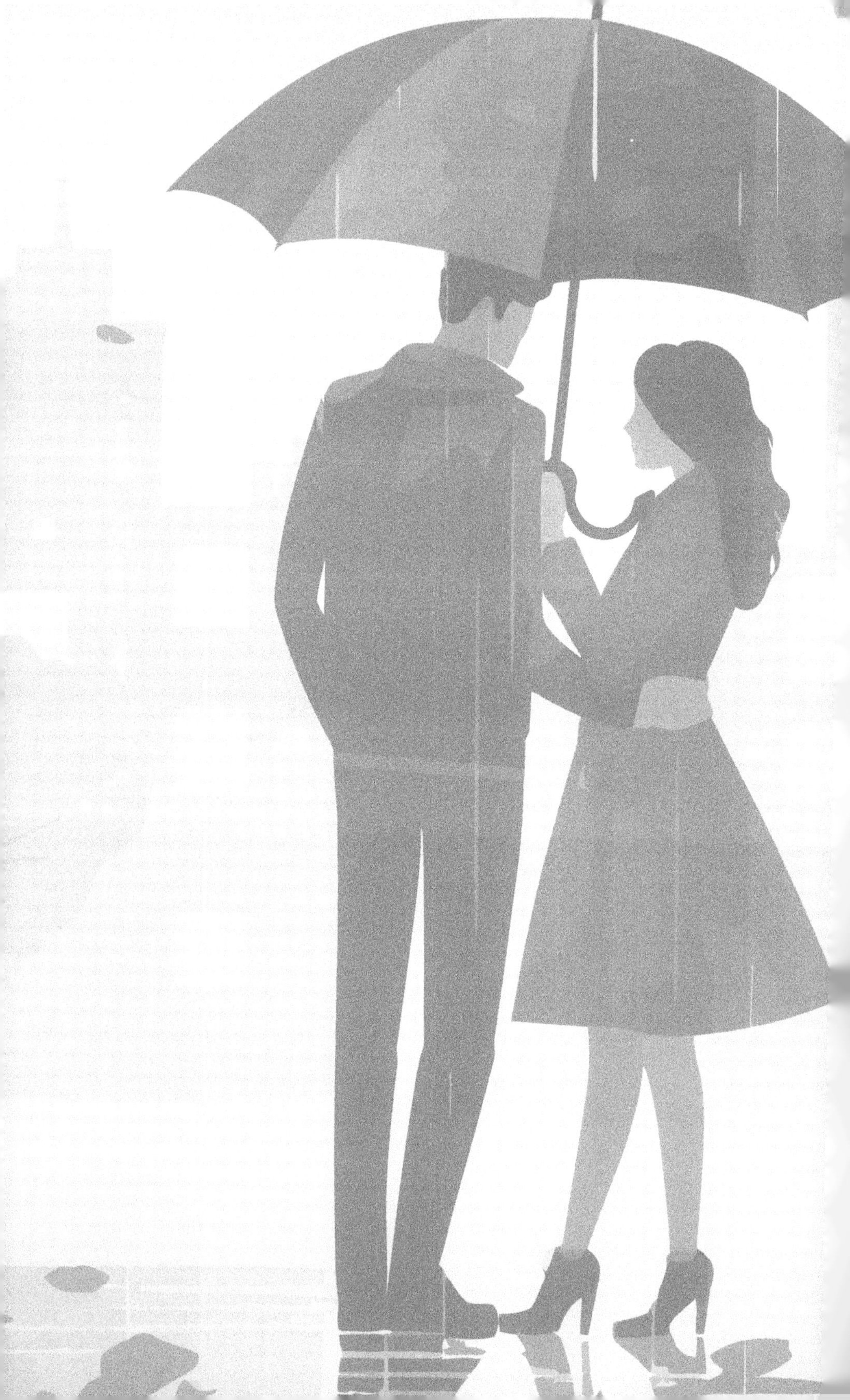

Chapter Thirty-Seven

JAMES

Two hours later, the only evidence of the thunder storm were the puddles on the sidewalks and the droplets on surfaces, specifically benches.

Tori and I walked downtown, ate pizza in a little pizza parlor with loud music and the buzz of conversation all around us.

It felt right. Normal.

But things were different now.

Maybe guys didn't usually think that life changed with a kiss, but I did. If I was the anomaly, then I was okay with that.

She was my girl. She'd always been my girl. And kissing her vanished any doubt I had left about it.

Her lips were swollen from kissing and her hair had that slightly mussed look that came from me tangling my hands in her long soft hair. She didn't even know her hair was mussed. It she did, she would have pulled it back and that would have been a loss.

I caught a couple of guys glancing at us. They'd look at her, then look at me. One gave a knowing little nod.

Yep. My girl. And they knew it.

When Tori smiled at me, I saw the girl I had loved all those years ago. An innocent girl with a pretty smile and bright eyes.

She looked the same to me. Time simply folded in on itself and the years vanished.

Whatever had happened between then and now no longer mattered.

After dinner, we walked hand in hand back along the edge of the lake with moonlight spilling over us, the water lapping softly at the edge of the beach.

In the distance beyond, sitting high on a knoll, the Grand Hotel stood sentinel over its island. In the end, the island belonged to the Grand Hotel and it knew it. The hotel knew it and the island knew it. Without the Grand Hotel, Mackinac Island would not be Mackinac Island.

"I wonder what it's like to live here," Tori said.

"I would think it would be wonderful in summer and cold in the winter."

"I don't mind the cold, especially if there's a warm fireplace and a good book."

I looked at her sideways. I could see her living her. I saw her clearly sitting in front of a warm fire on a cozy sofa, her laptop computer open. Teaching her classes online. Reading in the evenings.

If I looked closely enough, I could even see myself there with her. Wearing reading glasses as I read a book of my own.

In my vision, both of us had silver in our hair, but she would color hers away, keeping it dark brown.

"What are you thinking?" she asked.

"I'm thinking that it would be okay here until you wanted to go shopping or get your hair done. Then it could be a problem."

She laughed with a shrug. "I'm sure they have delivery services. Everybody shops online now."

"True."

"Somebody on this island does hair. If they don't then it's a missed opportunity for someone."

"Tori," I said. "I'm sorry I brought up Tiffany earlier. It wasn't right to bring you here to tell you that."

"It's okay," she said, but I heard the uncertainty in her voice.

I'd hurt her.

"You didn't know we'd end up staying here."

"Still. It was too much to put on you."

She stopped and looked out over the lake. Shoved her hair back with her free hand.

"I think you just needed to tell somebody," she said. "And you knew I was a good listener."

"No," I said. "It's not that. I could talk to Bella and I already talked to Mike about it."

"Who's Mike?"

"Friend of the family. The point is I didn't need to talk to you about it. I truly just wanted you to know. For you to make an informed decision."

"I'm a little confused about that. About what kind of decision I'm supposed to make."

Here in the magical moonlight of Mackinac Island, I realized I hadn't told her everything.

I had been just vague enough to make her confused.

"I meant it when I said I want to make things work this time."

She was looking at me with confusion mixed with hope.

"Tori," I said. "I want to make a life with you."

"Do you really mean that?"

I took both her hands and gazed deep into her eyes.

"You and I have something special. Something most people don't have in their lives."

The loud horn of the last ferry leaving the island filled the air.

"History?" she asked.

"Some of that. But so much more."

She nodded, her eyes bright with unshed moisture.

"We have a second chance," I said.

"Most people don't have that."

"Tori," I said. She was going to make me say it. She knew, but she wanted me to say it.

"Yes. A second chance. But more. You and I have a forever love."

She was looking at me, her eyes bright.

"Tori," I said. "It's you. It's always been you. It always will be."

"That thing you asked me about earlier," she said.

"Tiffany."

"Yes. Tiffany. Your baby."

"Maybe mine." I winced. "Maybe not. But yes. Tiffany."

"I don't care. I know I probably should. But I don't. I can't. I can't because it's you."

With a grin, I wrapped my arms around her lifted her off her feet.

"Promise me," I said.

"Okay."

"Promise me that nothing will come between us again. Not time. Not distance. No one. Exes. Mothers."

"I promise," she said. "Nothing will come between us."

We sealed that promise with a kiss.

No matter what, we had a forever love.

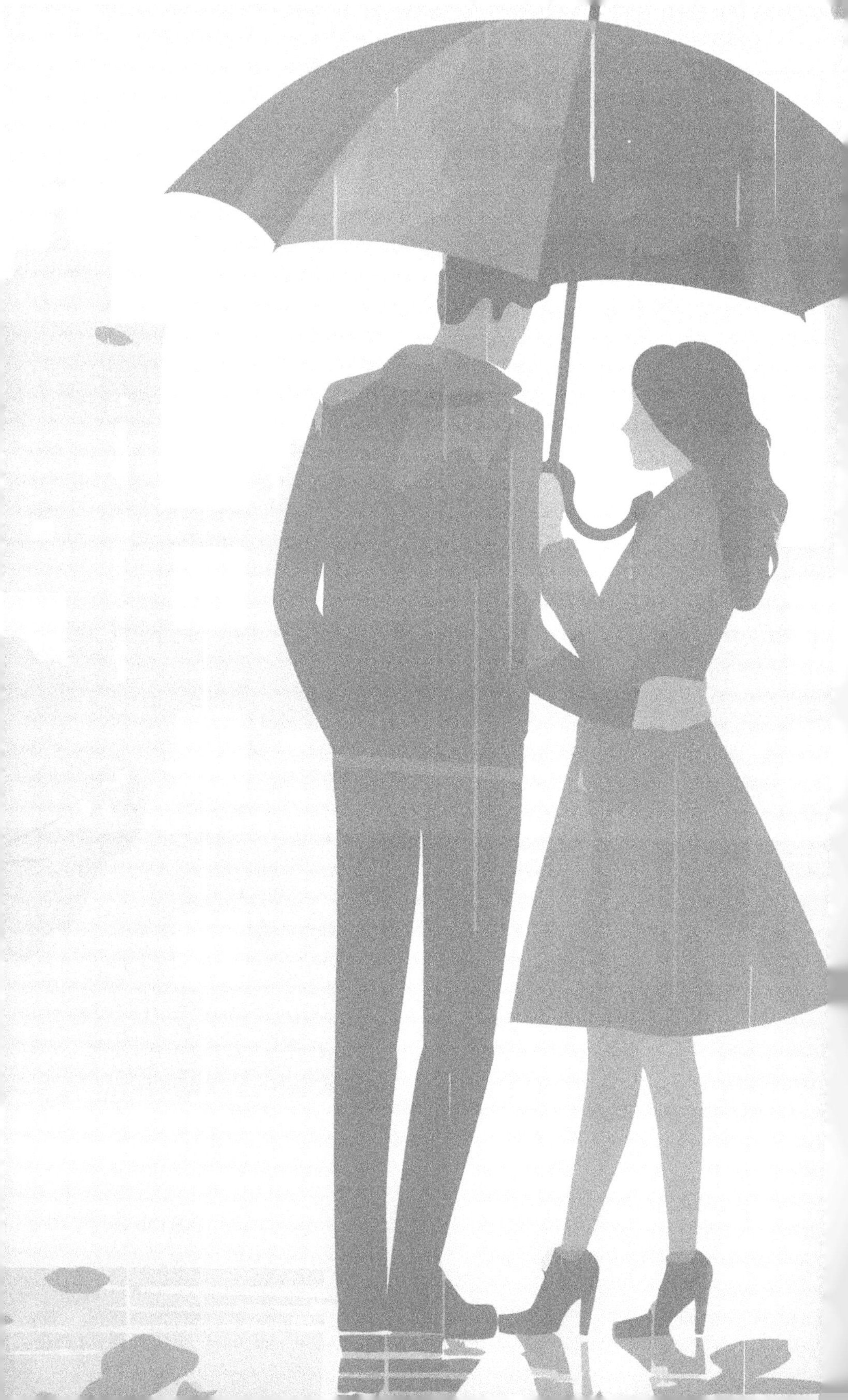

Epilogue

Victoria
November

THERE WAS something magical about the first snowfall of the season.

I watched from the window of the Ashton House.

Curled up in front of the fireplace on a big comfortable sectional, I had my laptop computer open and papers printed out all around me.

No one else was home today. That in itself was unusual. The large Ashton family all lived in the same house. The house was certainly big enough. Sometimes I still got lost.

Instead of the view from my tenth floor apartment, I had a view of the long driveway circling around to the main road. The road was lined with maple trees, limbs bare with winter, and spruce trees collecting snowflakes on their needles.

I didn't miss the high rise. I liked it here. I would, of course, like it anyplace James was.

I looked up as a truck came rumbling down the driveway.

My heart quickened as I realized it was James, coming home from his flight. I'd known he was on his way because he'd sent me a text, but it didn't keep me from loving it that he was home.

Knowing I wouldn't be able to concentrate, I closed my computer and picked up the cup of hot tea I had just made.

Coming in through the back door, he came straight to me.

Kissed me on the mouth, then, after I moved papers aside, sat down next to me.

"Hi," he said.

"Hi."

"End of the semester term papers?"

"I'll be awhile. There aren't that many of them, but they're actually good."

"Graduate students."

"That's right."

"Don't let me interrupt?"

"Too late," I said.

He sat back, his arms across the back of the sofa.

"It isn't Mackinac Island," he said.

"What do you mean?" I asked, breathing in the steam from the hot tea.

He just smiled.

"When you asked what it would be like to live on Mackinac, this is how I pictured you."

"Working?" I asked with a little smile.

"Partly," he said. "But relaxed on the sofa in front of the fireplace. Maybe it was here I'd pictured you all along."

"I like it here."

"I'm glad," he said. "It means you won't mind living here."

"You know I don't."

"So I have some news."

"I'm listening."

"Tiffany had her baby."

"Congratulations to her."

"I know."

"Did she ever tell you who the father is?"

"Yeah, but I don't know him."

"That's probably good," I said. "It could be weird if you did."

"Come here," he said, taking the mug out of my hands and pulling me into his lap.

"I've been wondering," he said. "Speaking of babies."

"Oh no."

"How many babies do you want to shoot for?"

"Are we having babies?"

He looked at me with mock shock.

"This house requires a person to have babies."

"Your brother doesn't have any." His youngest brother had been married for over a year.

"That's because he understands the pecking order."

I laughed.

"Why don't we just see what happens."

"Did I ever tell you that you aren't the normal girl?"

"I think you've always known that. It's one of the things you like about me, right?"

"I like everything about you."

He kissed me on the cheek. On the eyelids. On the lips.

"I like everything about you, too."

James and I had something very rare. We had a forever love.

It had just taken us a little while to come around to it. To make it stick.

But that was the thing about a forever love. It had always been there and it always would be.

AUTHOR OF PERFECTLY MISMATCHED

KATHRYN KALEIGH

Forever Vows

THE ASHTONS
FOREVER AND EVER

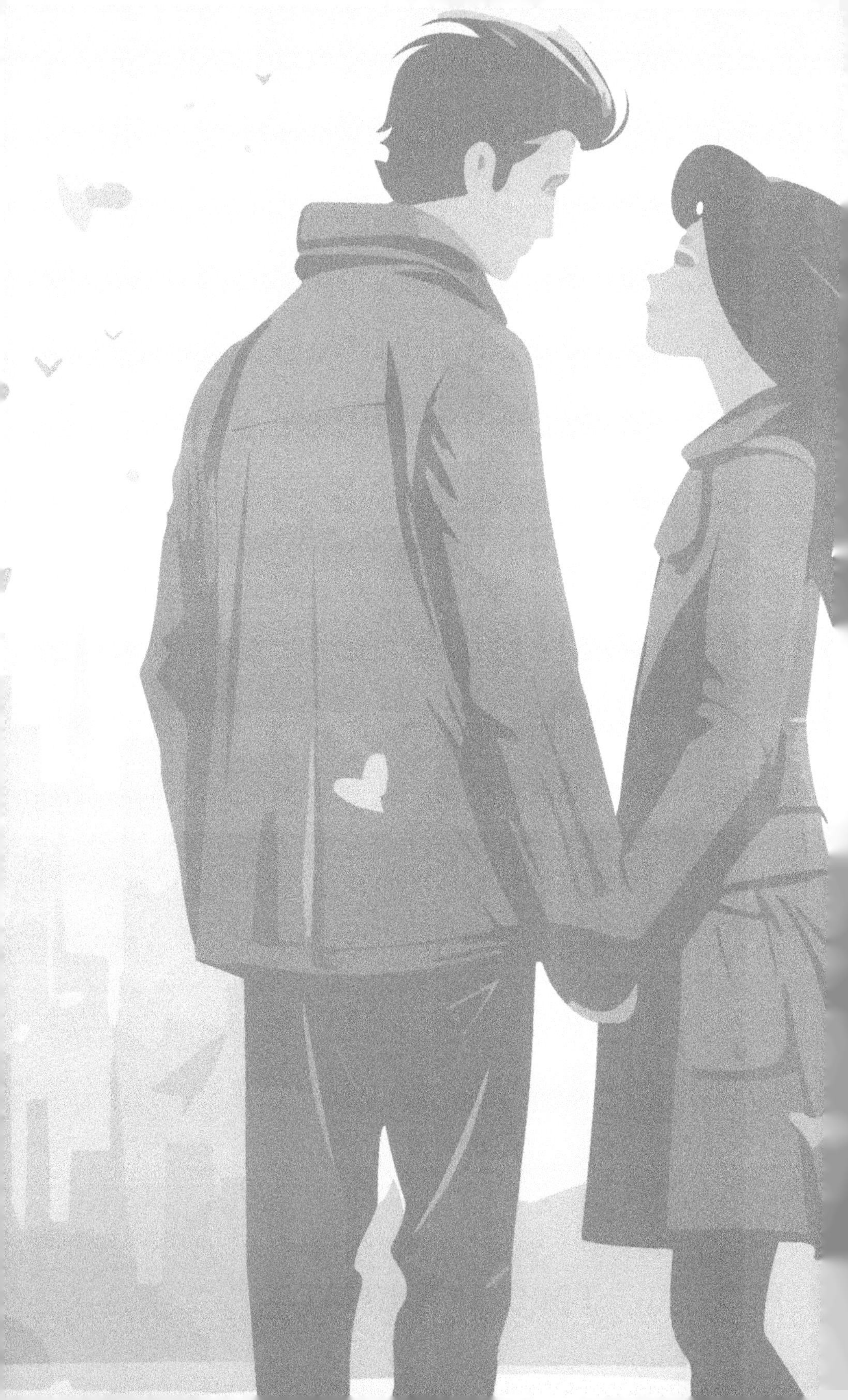

Preview
FOREVER VOWS

Prologue

Seventeen Years Ago

LITTLE BABY BIRDS hidden away in a straw nest tucked in the fork of the old maple tree chirped shrilly for their mother.

"Can you see them?" Isabella asked, standing on her toes as though that would make her taller than her four feet two inches. She bounced on her white sneakers, swinging her blonde ponytail in the process.

"Almost," nine-year-old Daniel said, swinging dangerously to land on the next limb. "There."

"What do you see?" Isabella asked.

"There are five of them," Daniel said, looking down, grinning from ear to ear.

"Five. Wow."

"No. Wait. There are six of them. They're starving."

Isabella glanced over her shoulder.

"Come down," she said. "Before the mother sees you."

"I'm not afraid of a bird," he said. "Let's get some worms. Feed them."

Isabella put her hands on her hips. "You can't feed the birds," she said. "Just take the picture and come down."

"You're bossy for a girl," Daniel said, but he took his phone out of his pocket and snapped a picture."

"Come down," she said, bouncing again.

"Okay. Okay."

Daniel scooted nimbly from one limb to the other and he made his way down.

"You're going to fall," Isabella said.

Daniel landed nimbly on his feet.

"Didn't fall," he said, holding his arms over his head.

"You're an idiot," Isabella said, but she blew out a breath of relief.

"Your idiot," he said.

"Not mine."

"Wait. You said you'd be my girlfriend."

"That was before I found out you're an idiot."

She turned, facing the warmth of the sunshine on her face.

"Do you want to see the picture or not?"

"Yes!" She turned back, smiling. "Let me see."

"Girls," Daniel muttered under his breath, but he held up his phone.

Isabella took the phone and zoomed in on the little baby birds, their mouths wide open.

"Aw," she said. "They're really hungry."

"I told you."

The flutter of wings above signaled the return of the mother bird.

"She's back," Isabella said.

"Let's go," Daniel grabbed her arm to lead her away.

"But—"

"If she knows we're here, she won't feed them."

"Why, that's the silliest thing—"

But Daniel pulled her away where they crouched behind a purple blooming hydrangea bush.

"How do we know she's feeding them?" Isabella asked, worried now about the mother bird knowing Daniel had been in the tree. "Do you think she smells you?"

But Daniel, an always prepared boy scout, pulled his spyglass out of his back pocket and zoomed in on the birds.

"Look," he said. "She's feeding them."

"Aw," she said. "She's sharing her food. That is so amazingly wonderful."

Daniel watched Isabella carefully.

Satisfied, she lowered the spyglass and smiled at him.

"We can have six babies if you want."

"What?"

"Babies." Daniel sat back on his heels. "After we're married, of course."

"You don't want to marry me," Isabella said.

"I do. I'll marry you right now."

Isabella looked at him crossly and crossed her arms.

"There's no priest here."

"We don't need a priest. My sister said all you need to do is to say your vows."

"How does she know that?"

"She learned it in history class."

Isabella didn't really believe him. She had an older sister and three older brothers. If that was a thing, she would have heard about it.

But Daniel said it with the utmost conviction. And besides. He was looking at her with those smiling blue eyes that made her heart beat too fast.

"How?" Isabella asked, curiosity overcoming skepticism.

Daniel seemed to think for a minute.

"You don't know—"

"Put your hands in mine," he said holding out his hands, palms up.

She put her hands in his.

"Now what?"

"We say our vows." He took a breath. "I do."

Isabella had never been to a wedding, but she had seen weddings on television. So far, it seemed right to her. Right enough anyway.

"I do," she said. "So we're married now?"

"Not yet," he said. "There's one more thing we have to do to make it official."

"What's that?"

"I have to kiss you."

Isabella's eyes widened. Daniel Benton was going to kiss her.

"Are you sure?" She had imagined this moment about two million times. Since Kindergarten.

"If we don't, we won't be married."

Well, Isabella thought, she had come this far. Mimicking what she had seen on television, she closed her eyes, leaned forward at the waist, and puckered her lips.

Seconds passed. Two seconds. Three seconds.

Maybe she had misunderstood.

But then Daniel's lips lightly touched hers.

Opening her eyes, she grinned at him.

"We're married now."

"Yes," he said. "Forever and ever."

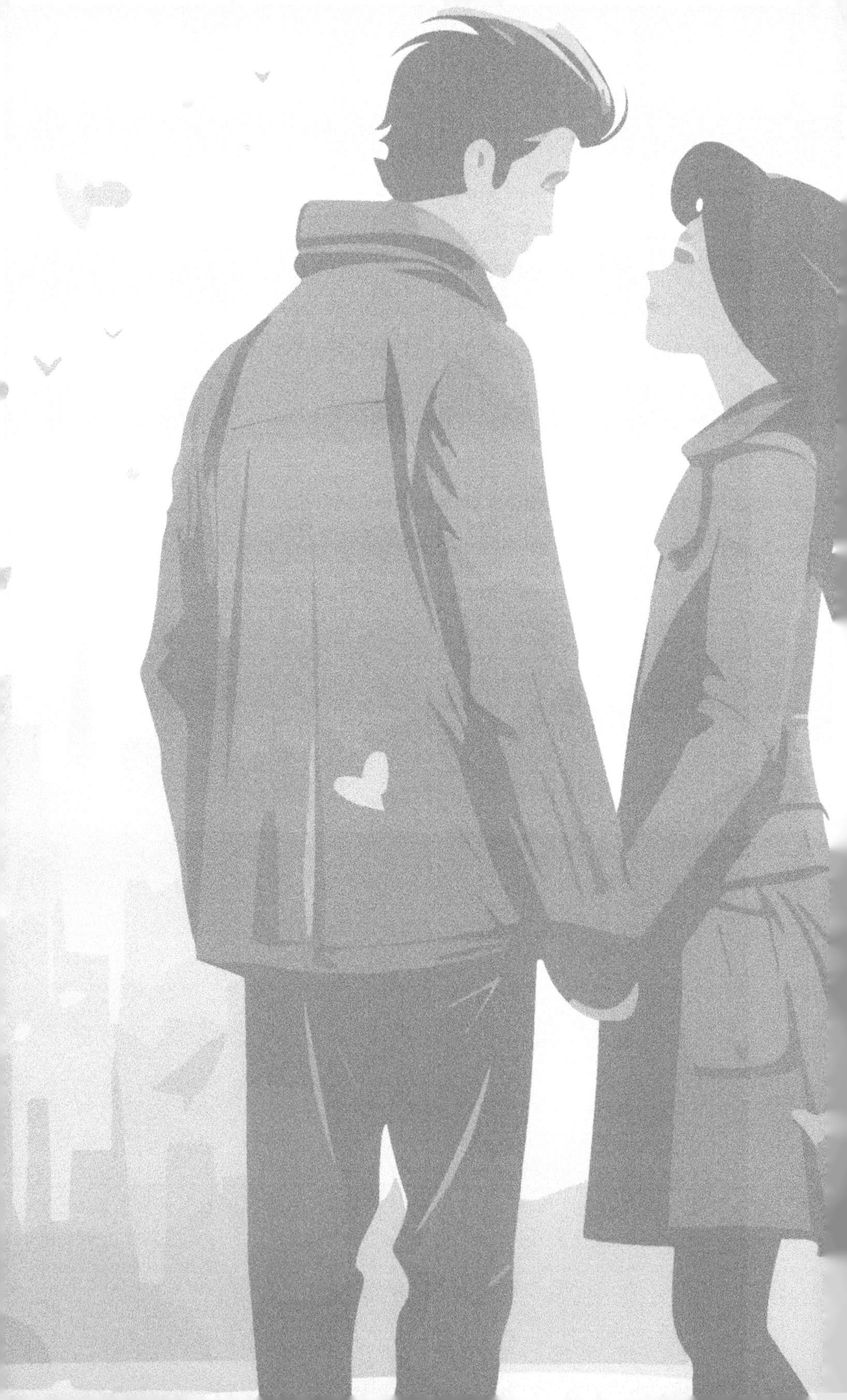

Preview
FOREVER VOWS

Chapter 1
Isabella Ashton

Today

I UNROLLED the oversized vellum graph paper, spread it over the drafting table, and clipped it onto the top edge to keep it from sliding off.

Early morning sunlight streamed in through the third floor window of Ashton Manor, casting a bright glow of light across the desk.

My new studio. A quiet place just for me to work.

Maybe a little too quiet. I tapped my phone, turning on some popular music just loud enough to fill in some of that background quietness. Coming from a crowded corporate office environment, I had to get myself accustomed to the quiet.

Not quite happy with the light, I shoved the heavy hardwood desk, just a little, shifting it so that the paper was free from shadows.

The drafting table was new, but the desk behind me where I kept my rulers, pencils, paper, and other supplies was antique. It made a good desk for my computer, too.

The antique desk stayed put. It was so heavy, I couldn't move it if I had to.

It had been handed down through the years and according to my grandmother it had been built in the early 1800s and used by my great great great great grandfather who had built this house. She also told me that it had a secret compartment.

There were lots of stories about what was in that secret compartment, but no one knew for sure.

Everyone looked for the secret compartment. I looked for it, too. But no one could find it. I wasn't giving up on it. Someday I was going to figure it out.

On the lawn below, my sister-in-law's black retriever, basically a big oversized puppy, had been sniffing around for half an hour. Suddenly lifting his head, he raced toward the line of maple trees that indicated the end of the lawn and the beginning of the forest, toward something only he could see.

The dog came to an abrupt skidding stop at the edge of the lawn, about fifty yards across, at the maple trees, with their bright red leaves of fall, and laid his ears back.

Tori, the dog's owner, called him back. Biscuit. Tori and my brother James named their dog Biscuit. What happened to normal dog names like Charlie, Buddy, or Rover. Spot. Spot was a good name for a dog. Especially Biscuit since he had a white spot between his eyes.

If I had a dog, I'd name him Spot. Or maybe Bandit. Depending.

Personally, I was more of cat person. My best friend had a cat named Fluffy. A normal pet with a normal pet name.

Biscuit raced back toward the house on long gangly legs and disappeared beneath the terrace deck.

The back door closed below as they came inside.

With no more distractions outside, I sat on my drafting stool and sipped my hot latte.

Running a hand over the pristine sheet of paper, I considered where I wanted to start.

I had a rough sketch on a napkin. Something had come to me while I was having Sunday dinner with my family and instead of looking for sheet of real paper, I'd used the napkin at hand.

That's how it worked for me.

Ideas occurred to me when I was not supposed to be working—like Sundays with my family or showers. I got most of my ideas when I showered. Something about the hot water flowing over my head tended to loosen my thoughts.

The Ashton Manor was more than a house. It was an estate. I lived here with my parents, my four older siblings, and two sisters-in-law.

The house was so big we only saw each other in passing.

It would probably be different now, though, I mused, because starting today, I would be working from home.

Tori also worked from home, but she didn't have a studio. She liked working downstairs on the sectional sofa in front of the fireplace.

I'd worked on the kitchen table until today, but that had been when I'd worked from home after putting in hours at my full-time job.

I still couldn't believe I'd turned in my resignation and left my corporate job to go off on my own.

I was going on a leap of faith.

Doubling down on my idea of designing small cottage home offices for individuals. With so many people, professionals, working from home now, I saw the need for people having their own office space just steps away from their back doors.

A place they could call their own whether they wanted to work in the quiet or attend a Zoom meeting without the noises of family interrupting.

I'd only sold one of my plans, but I'd gotten a lot of interest.

Since it aligned with what I wanted to do, I took the leap.

One of my cousins out of Houston had put together a business plan for me. Ran some numbers.

And the result had been startling.

And yet I had not made the decision lightly.

I made pretty good money working at my corporate job. Decent, steady money.

But if my business made a go of it, I could make in one month what I would make in one year. My cousin had cautioned me that business success did not happen overnight.

I knew that, of course.

I also knew that at twenty-six, I had to make a move if I was going to.

So many people at my job were trapped. They had mortgages and car notes and children. They had too many obligations to leave the steady work force.

I'd personally spoken to a dozen people at work. They all told me the same thing.

If they had it to do over again, they would go out on their own before they became dependent on the money. I knew that ninety-nine percent of them would not do anything differently.

People tended not to take risks like that. They preferred the benefits and pension plan and steady income.

I had a safety net most people didn't have.

I had a place to live and no expenses.

My parents wouldn't let me fail. I might have to pivot, but I wouldn't fail. My grandfather owned several high rise buildings in Pittsburgh and establishments inside those buildings including five star restaurants. He provided the capital and other people ran the businesses.

He was exceptionally successful. His brother, my Uncle Noah, was also an entrepreneur. Uncle Noah had created the largest and most successful private airline company from the ground up. Skye Travels.

He had airplanes housed at various places around the country, including Pittsburgh.

That was my goal. I wanted to have my own architect firm with people working for me around the country. Or at least maybe in an office in the city.

I had entrepreneurship in my blood.

But first I had to start with my second blueprint.

I had to establish a brand before I could make sales. A lot of people thought it went the other way around. Most people wanted to find a client before they made blueprints.

I knew I had to have blueprints to attract clients, at least at first.

People had to see what they were buying, especially from someone without an established track record.

That would be me.

But if determination had anything to do with it, I would have lots of blueprints for people to choose from. I'd have a website that I'd already been working on. All I had to do now was to make the designs and put them up for sale.

I was betting on myself.

My phone chimed with a text message.

> Unknown number
>
> Hello. Isabella Ashton? I got your number from your neighbor. She said you might could held me design an office cottage for me.

My heart pounded rapidly in my chest.

This was happening much more quickly than I had planned.

Staring at the blank sheet of paper in front of me wasn't going to get the job done.

> Can we meet? To talk about what you have in mind.

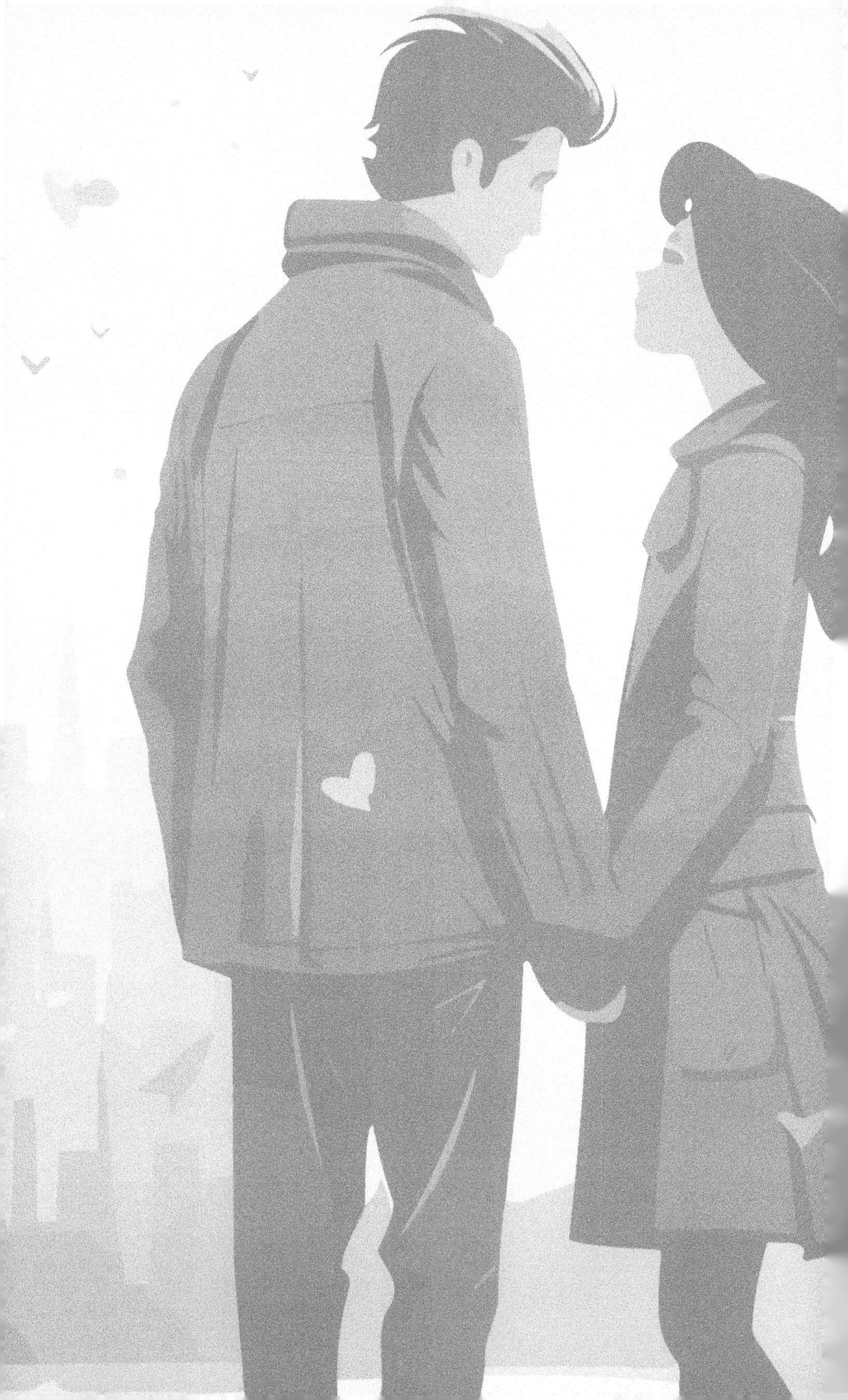

Preview

FOREVER VOWS

Chapter 2
Daniel Benton

I STEPPED off the elevator onto the second floor of the Skye Travels building at the edge of the Houston airport tarmac and turned toward Noah Worthington's office.

The thick carpet muffled the sound of my shoes. The offices were quiet. The only noise came from outside. The airplane engine on one side and the freeway traffic on the other side.

Noah Worthington was what I thought of as the big boss.

Didn't get much bigger in my mind.

Noah had started Skye Travels with one little Cessna airplane and built it into the largest private airline company in the country. He now had a fleet of airplanes including more Phenoms than any other one single man owned. Most of them were housed in Houston, but some were housed in various places around the country including Whiskey Springs and Mackinac Island. He had a tendency to go for places off the beaten path. Beautiful, magical places that didn't have easy access.

Of course, he also had airplanes in other cities, too, like Dallas and Birmingham.

Maggie, talking on her headset, as always, held up a hand in greeting as I passed. Maggie had been with Skye Travels for years. Some claimed she came with the place but Maggie always evaded giving a straight answer about that.

I walked down the hallway and stopped at Noah's door.

He turned around from where he stood looking out over the tarmac. He had the best view of the Houston Airport from here. He could see every one of his private jets as they came and went and if that wasn't enough, he could watch commercial jets landing and taking off on nearby runways. Most of them went airborne right over his office.

It was a befitting office for a man of Noah's stature and reputation.

I'd worked for Skye Travels for five years coming here straight after college graduation. The envy of most of my peers, many of whom took me off their friend list. It was my fault I landed one of the most coveted jobs for pilots.

Fortunately, I had friends who weren't pilots. I just didn't stay in touch nearly as much as I should.

"Come in," Noah said. "Have a seat."

In the five years that I had worked here at Skye Travels, I had never been summoned to his office. He'd interviewed me back when and that was that. I'd only seen him in passing since, at the office at least.

I'd been to his home for a couple of normal Sunday dinners and I'd been to holiday parties.

But I'd never once been summoned to his office.

If I had done something wrong, I couldn't imagine what it would be.

As I took a seat on the sofa in his little sitting area, a large commercial jet came in for a landing, the loud roar from its engines filling the air.

Noah didn't even seem to notice. He took two bottles of water from a little refrigerator and handed one to me. The water bottles had the red Skye Travels logo on the label.

"Thank you," I said, twisting the top off and drinking while I waited for him to fill me in on what he needed to talk to me about.

I shifted in my seat and adjusted my tie.

"You're not in trouble," Noah said, watching me.

Had I been that obvious?

"Good to know," I said.

"Actually I need a favor."

"A favor." I had not expected Noah Worthington to need a favor from me. I tended to fly beneath the radar.

Just doing my job and going home.

But I was a pilot and it was hard for a pilot to fly beneath the radar for very long.

"Sure thing," I said. "How can I help?"

I was thinking maybe he needed me to take an extra flight. Maybe an overnight flight. The married guys didn't like the extended overnight trips and Noah tried to accommodate them.

Being single, I didn't mind taking overnight trips, but he would know that. I took overnight trips all the time.

"You're originally from Pittsburgh, right?"

"Yes sir." I was still trying to figure out what kind of favor he might be looking for.

"Good," he said, stopping to watch one of his planes takeoff. He probably even knew who the pilot was. How many times had he watched me land and takeoff?

I waited in silence. He'd tell me in his own good time.

"I need someone to cover one of my Phenoms up there for a while."

"Pittsburgh?"

"Yes." He toyed with the label on his bottle of water.

"Okay. How long?"

"Two months."

"Oh. Two months."

I had an apartment. I had a little succulent that I'd had for ages. But I didn't have a girlfriend and I had a feeling he somehow knew that.

Noah knew everything there was to know about his people. Even those of us who stayed below the radar.

"You'll be provided an apartment and a car. All expenses covered."

I didn't doubt that.

"Why me?"

Noah smiled at me. An older man with silver in his hair, he still held himself tall and straight and could have passed for a much younger man.

In that smile, I could see the charm and persuasiveness that had no doubt helped him obtain the level of success he had achieved.

"Since you're from there," he said. "I thought you wouldn't mind using the opportunity to go back. Spend some time with family."

Family. I still had a grandmother who lived in Pittsburgh, but my parents had retired to Florida. He would know that, of course.

A little tendril of fear wound its way through me.

"Has someone contacted you about my grandmother?" I asked, fearing the worst. Someone could have contacted me here about her. Not likely, but possible.

I should call her more often. She lived alone and as far as I knew there was no one to look in on her.

"No. No," Noah said, looking at me with concern now. "But it sounds like maybe you're thinking you might want to see how she's doing. If you decide to help me out on this."

"Of course," I said, scrubbing my chin. "I'd be happy to help you out."

"Good," Noah said. "That's good."

"I'll look in on my grandmother while I'm there."

Noah laughed.

"I'm sure she'll be happy to see you. Maggie will get you all the details."

With that, he stood up and walked back to the window."

"Is that all you needed, Mr. Worthington?"

"That's all," he said. "Thank you for helping out."

Still reeling from the strange conversation with the big boss, I went in search of Maggie.

My grandmother might be the only official family I had in Pittsburgh, but she wasn't the only person I had left behind.

Noah had really given me no choice.

I would be spending the next two months in my hometown.

Pittsburgh.

I was going home to Pittsburgh.

Not a big deal, I told myself. I would just take my plant with me. I could leave my car here at the airport in the Skye Travels parking lot.

I had lots of arrangements to make, but I was used to traveling on the fly.

I was a pilot. it's what I did.

Going back to Pittsburgh, though. That was not something I'd planned on doing.

First things first, I'd call Liam, my friend from college. Last I heard, he still lived in Pittsburgh.

The thought of spending two months there with no one to talk to but my grandmother didn't sound like something I wanted to do.

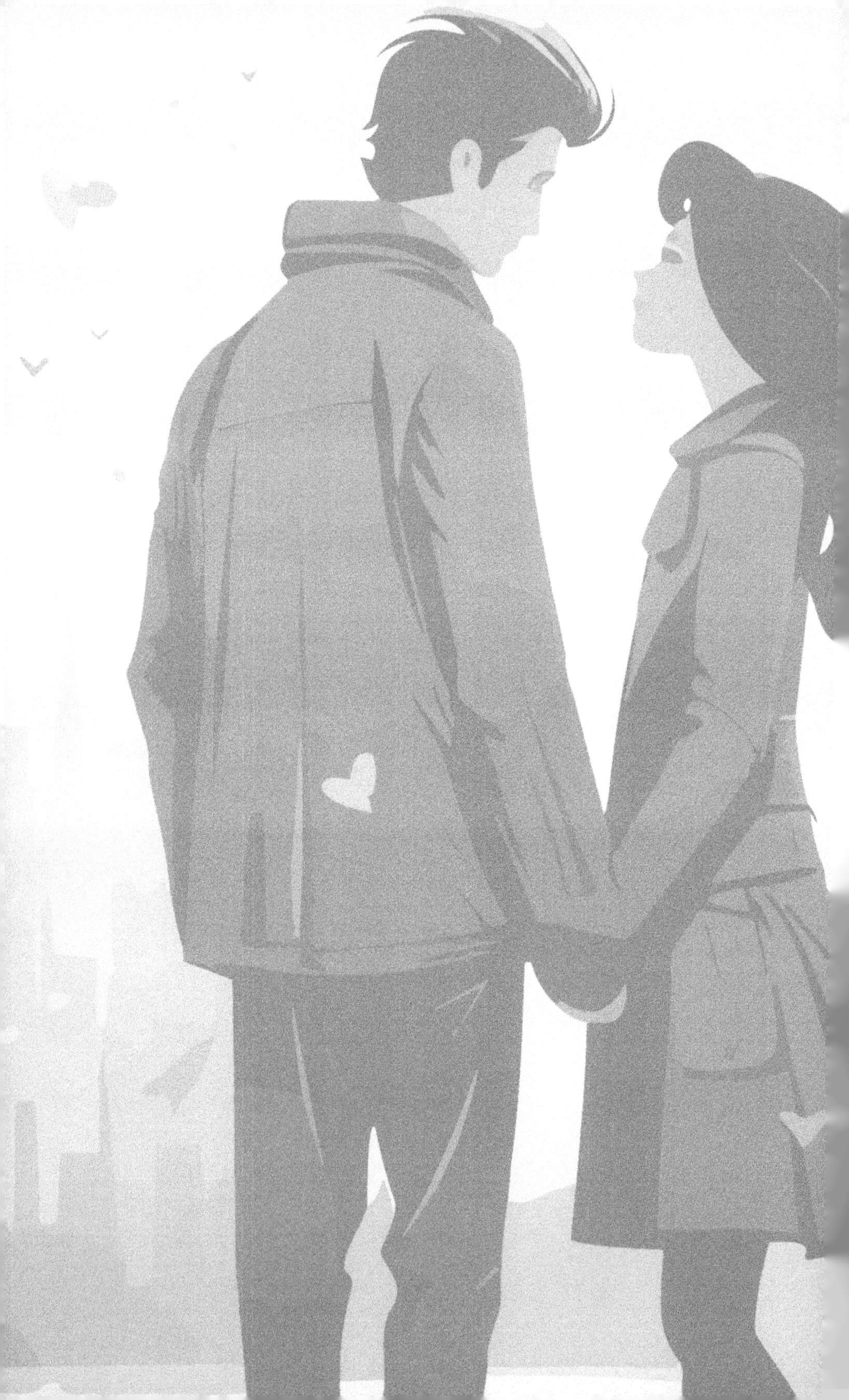

Preview

FOREVER VOWS

**Chapter 3
Isabella**

I RECOGNIZED the name of my new client—my first private client—but I didn't recognize the address or the house.

The house was a large Georgian colonial-style house with what I thought of as a flat front. As an architect, I had a love hate relationship with the style. I loved it because it was iconic and symmetrical. All American.

Two stories. Two windows on either side. Kitchen in the back.

I hated it—too strong a word really—because as an architect, it was difficult to design something in that style that stood out from the crowd.

It was hard to create something different out of a classic design.

The house was freshly washed, letting the pale white brick shine through, belying its age.

Using the thick iron knocker, I knocked on the door and waited. A baby cried in the background and toddler screeched.

Maybe there was more than one Liam Johnson in Pittsburgh. It was more than a little bit possible. Likely.

The blonde woman who opened the front door had hair falling out of her ponytail. She looked harried and stressed, but she smiled at me.

I knew this woman. Somehow. I wasn't sure yet. But I knew her.

"Hi," she said and hearing her voice everything fit together and I recognized her.

"Hi." I smiled. "Melissa?"

"Yes?" With a toddler holding onto her right leg, she frowned at me with a mix of confusion and uncertainty.

"I'm Isabella Ashton," I said. "You contacted me or maybe your husband did."

"Isabella." Her face brightened. "The architect."

"Yes."

"Come in." I stepped inside after she opened the door. "I think... I think I know you." She watched me intently, trying to figure it out.

"You married Liam Johnson, right?" She nodded. "Your boyfriend was best friends with my... friend Daniel."

"Oh, of course," she said. "I have baby brain. I should have put that together."

"How would you?" I asked, giving her a break. From the looks of her house, she needed one.

"Come back to the kitchen," she said. "I have beanie weenies on the stove."

"People still eat those?" I mused.

"Three-year-olds do. I don't know about people."

I laughed.

"Have a seat," she said, picking up a teddy bear from one of the dining room chairs and setting it on top of the table.

As I sat down, she went back to the stove in the center of the island where she was stirring what did indeed smell like beanie weenies.

"I'm actually the one who contacted you."

"Oh. You work from home?" I tried to imagine Melissa getting any work done from anywhere, especially from here.

Besides the toddler attached to her leg, she had one in a playpen and if I was any judge at all, she had another one on the way.

She disentangled the toddler off her leg and set her in the dining room chair next to me.

The little girl looked at me as though she had never seen another human before.

"Hi," I said, getting no response.

"You design work cottages?" she asked, taking a pack of weenies from the refrigerator and proceeding to chop them into bite sized pieces.

"Yes," I said, gladly turning my attention back to Melissa. "I just —" I bit my tongue as I started to tell her that I had just started.

My mentor's words rang in my head. "Never let them know that you're new at what you do. As far as clients know, you are the expert."

She looked at me questioningly.

"I just wasn't sure what you all were looking for." I smiled.

"Liam doesn't know I contacted you," she said.

"Oh. I see." I didn't, but I would.

She slid the weenies off the cutting board and stirred them in with the beans.

"Liam is an attorney."

"Right. I remember he studied law."

"He has an office downtown, but he also does a lot of work from home." She glanced around. "I think he would do a lot more work at home if it was a little quieter." She lowered her voice as she neared the end of her sentence.

I glanced at the little girl. She was still watching me in silence.

"Hence the cottage office," I said. I hadn't decided for sure what I was going to call my little home office buildings, but right now cottage office seemed to fit.

"Yes," she said, enthusiastically. "Anything to keep my man at home, you understand?"

"Of course." Never let them know you're new and never let them know you didn't have a man.

She dipped up a spoonful of beanie weenies and put them on a blue plastic plate. Set it in front of the little girl.

"Do you want some beanie weenies?" she asked. "We have plenty."

"No," I said quickly, "but thank you."

Melissa put a scoop of beanie weenies on another saucer and sat down at the table with it.

"Eat," she told the little girl, then proceeded to do so herself.

"Sorry to eat in front of you," she said. "But I have a Zoom call in thirty minutes.

"No need to apologize," I said, fascinated at not only seeing an adult eating beanie weenies, but also that the little girl did as she was told.

Being the youngest of five siblings, I didn't know a whole lot about children, but Melissa made chaos look easy.

"How much space are you thinking?" I asked, glancing out the back window at what, from here, looked like a massive back yard. Plenty of room to put a cottage office.

"I don't know," Melissa said with a little shrug.

I didn't remember her being so laid back in college. Maybe having two and a half children did that to a person.

"Can you put together some designs? You know. A starting place? And we can go over them from there?"

"Of course. I didn't bring anything today. I was just hoping to get a general idea of size and scope."

Melissa finished off her beanie weenies. Took the plate to the sink, rinsed it, and put it in the dishwasher.

"Just think attorney," she said.

"Will he have clients come here?"

"Maybe," she said. "Probably. A lot of Zoom calls, but clients might come here."

I was wondering if maybe she shouldn't ask him, but she obviously wanted it to be a surprise. I would use what information I had to start with.

"I can pay you by the hour," she said. "What's your rate?"

Fortunately, I was prepared to answer that question. I told her my rate.

"Okay," she said without a blink. I had been afraid that it was a little high. I was asking more per hour than I had made at my corporate job. All at the advice of my cousin in Houston.

"Just text me an invoice. I'll pay you for today. I really have to get ready for my call. When can you come back?"

I opened up my calendar app. My time was wide open, but I didn't tell her that. I calculated how much time I would need to put together the first outline of a sketch.

"I have time Friday afternoon," I said.

"Perfect. Text me if you have any questions between now and then."

"Do you mind if I use the back door so I can get a feel for the space?"

"Not at all," she said. "That's a great idea. There's a stone walkway that leads around to the front."

She somehow managed to herd me to the door without it feeling like I was being dismissed, although I was.

"I'll see you on Friday," she said.

Feeling like I had just been through a whirlwind, I stood outside the back door of the colonial style house, the door closed behind me and tried to regroup.

So my client was the Liam Johnson I had known from college... or rather his wife.

I hadn't considered that I would be designing a surprise cottage office for someone. That added a whole different level to things.

Even more levels came from knowing the clients. Or more specifically from knowing them when they were college students.

I wouldn't let that affect anything though.

I considered the space they had for the building. Imagined the little cottage tucked among the maple trees.

A lot of people would want to cut trees to make a clean area to build. I didn't believe in that. I would work around the trees. Let them stand.

Maybe even find a way to bring the outdoors inside.

The beauty of it was if the Johnsons didn't like the design, I could sell it to someone else. And on top of that, I would get paid for putting together the design.

That was unexpected and nice.

I took a few photographs. Some mental measurements. There was plenty of room to work with.

When I came back Friday, I would bring a tape measure and do some actual measurements.

Using the stone walkway to make my way around front, I considered that they already had a built-in entrance for clients. Clients wouldn't even have to go inside the main house. I imagined a little sign out front with Liam's name, instructed them to follow an understated arrow.

Considering the chaos created by children in there, that was most definitely a good thing.

This was good.

A very good challenge.

Keep Reading Forever Vows...

Kathryn Kaleigh writes sweet contemporary romance, time travel romance, and historical romance.

kathrynkaleigh.com

Milton Keynes UK
Ingram Content Group UK Ltd.
UKHW020344240824
447235UK00004B/237